ONE
KIND
FAVOR

Also by Kevin McIlvoy

A Waltz
The Fifth Station
Little Peg
Hyssop
The Complete History of New Mexico
57 Octaves Below Middle C
At the Gate of All Wonder

ONE KIND FAVOR

a novel

KEVIN McILVOY

wtaw press

Published by WTAW Press
PO Box 2825
Santa Rosa, CA 95405
www.wtawpress.org

One Kind Favor is a satirical work of fiction committed by a fraudulent, lying,
hypocritical, faithless, shameless, bigoted, poisonous, misogynist, arrogant,
traitorous, ignorant criminal author assaulting the nation he sees in his mirror.

Edited by Peg Alford Pursell
Cover art *Moon Frost* by Kevin McIlvoy
Designed by HR Hegnauer

Library of Congress Cataloging-in-Publication Data

Names: McIlvoy, Kevin, 1953-, author.
Title: One kind favor : a novel / Kevin McIlvoy
Description: Santa Rosa, CA: WTAW Press, 2021.
Identifiers: LCCN: 2020940171 | ISBN: 978-1-7329820-3-1 (pbk.) |
            978-1-7329820-4-8 (eBook)
Subjects: LCSH Lynching--Fiction. | Race relations--Fiction. | Racism--Fiction.
| Hate crimes--Fiction. | Murder--Fiction. | North Carolina--Fiction. | BISAC
FICTION / General
Classification: LCC PS3563.C369 O54 2021 | DDC 813.54--dc23

WTAW Press is a not-for-profit literary press. We are grateful for the assistance
we receive from individual donors.

Manufactured in the United States of America and printed on acid-free paper.

In memory of North Carolina victims
of racial violence or injustice, past and present.

There's one kind favor I'll ask of you:
please see that my grave is kept clean.

Blind Lemon Jefferson

PART I

1.

Naming matters here in Cord, which was once called Chord and, before that, Curd.

The most prominent business in town is the combined bar and consignment shop owned first by Minister Stanley and next by Miss Acker and last by Junior Stanley. Rather than make a fresh sign, Miss Acker added her name when she was the new owner. When Junior took over he crossed her name through and added his. Reflecting no hard feelings, the sign, Stanley's~~Acker's~~Stanley's, told the story just fine. Eventually, Miss Acker was manager of the consignment, Junior was manager of the bar, and Minister Stanley was the all-around staffer. For generations of locals, Stanley's~~Acker's~~Stanley's has been a place of escape—every community has such rabbit holes—for those of us wishing to be ourselves and trueselves and otherselves.

If you were a new regular, you were called "Reg" until people knew the name you wanted to go by.

We understood that white Presences and Black Presences were regulars, that they stayed, returned, were never gone long. We have known about the Presences since the race murders here, one hundred and fifty years of them; and since the time when Civil War Confederates and their descendents settled in this area; and since the first slaves arrived in chains and were assigned to tobacco or cotton farms, renamed, reassigned, resold; and since the years when Reconstruction cynically redefined the term "free citizen."

During the period since the Voting Rights Act, we have begrudgingly accepted the place-name that does not appear on the town welcome sign. Exactly at the beginning of the Obama administration, our white population here first began to openly take pride in the specific designation, "Crackertown."

The Klan dead are here, and the living Klan is here. The dead NRA that values life and the living NRA that values profit is here. The Jim Crow Democrat dead are here, and the living Jim Crow and Jesus Crow jackboot white supremacists are here. The dead election-riggers, so quiet but so brazen, are here; the living election-riggers, granted permission by the US Supreme Court on June 25, 2013, pay cash to buy election results that favor Trumpublicans who cannot win office without subverting the voting franchise. The war dead are here, and the living civilians and veterans who honor them are here, and here are the happy witnesses to the draft-dodging, illegitimate president spitting on the stones and into the open graves.

Defending family and community against minority rights, the Southern Baptists here became the official religion of American apartheid before sesquicentenially healing declining church enrollments through racial reconciliation, then, late in the twentieth century, beginning their relentless effort to defend family and community against the rights of transgender and gay people and the autonomy of women and the safety of refugee children and families. The United Methodist Church's soul-dead believers in old-school religious fundamentalism speak their poison words here, and the louder and louder homunculus Word of Faith cult and cults like it grow from the evangelical spore.

The moneyed who died sucking the poor dry are here sucking Koch and Pope, and more of the Kochsuckers and the SuckPopes and Mercernaries are here than ever before, now that the redhats rule us, blood and soil.

2.

During every evening of the first week of November 2016, Acker and Woolman and Lincoln, a trio of troublemakers, splashed around in the inflatable children's pool they had filled from the spigot behind the HH Inn. (Acker called it the Helltel.) The air was cool that time of year, so people had their windows open. Some of our townsfolk, particularly ones living in the Dowless Place trailer park, could hear the racket the three made, and on the last evening of the foolishness they did not waste time warning Lincoln to quit.

Ignoring Woolman and Acker, they shouted to the young Black high school student by name. From the protection of night, they said, "Your people don't want you fouling up like this, you know, Lincoln," and "You trying to piss us off?" And one of them said, "Lincoln, what do you think you know other niggers don't?"

Acker said, "Join us, fuckers," and standing up as if to flaunt her naked body, added, "Show us your little pricks, Little Dicks."

Bunny and The Mister Rounceval, the couple who managed the Helltel, appeared through the darkness. The Mister said to the little pricks at their trailer windows, "Keep them in your pants." And Bunny, her dentures not sealed properly, said, "Liiittle beebee duckses, go beck to slip now."

The Mister said, "You just got this playpool?"

"Yep," said Lincoln. "You heard about our No Questions Asked campaign?"

"Guess that went okay." The Mister sat down near the round pool's yellow bumper and touched the pattern of patching and repatching.

He speculated that the pool held one hundred gallons at most. He liked their idea of removing stolen goods from guilty stealers, no questions asked. In 1931 he had stolen wool fingerless gloves from his grade school teacher's desk drawer, left side, carved scroll handle, screeching drawer skids, the whole class watching and Bunny, too; eight decades later, the crime made it possible for him to hold but not touch how he felt about the cruel Mrs. Straupitter.

Bunny took off her shoes and her support hose, set them on the grass, and she lifted her nightdress to her knees and stood in the pool and gazed a long time at the naked bodies of Woolman and Lincoln and longer yet at Acker, and she said, "You fith your bodthies good."

"Cold out here," said Woolman.

"Cold," said Lincoln.

Shouldn't Acker have said something?

"Go on in," said The Mister to the three. "Take the elevator and I'll follow." He didn't like the Inn's carpeted stairs to be wet. He knew that Bunny, terrified of the elevator, would not mind any damage to the tile floor.

Bunny stayed. The dark wildnesses of the night sky nested inside the pool. A spreading stain of gloom, a horngleam, a burring train sound. At the ensorcelling moment when she had begun to undress, she heard a dog splash into the water, and in came the dog's companion. Though she had never seen the man and dog, she knew them. Everyone in Cord knew them.

"Hello," she said.

The dog nosed her legs slightly apart, sniffed, sniffed the back of her knees, his tail weltering the water near her feet. He sniffed the driftage of Bunny, and the strong vape- and cologne-scent of Acker that remained in the air.

"Hello," she said, again unanswered.

The shifting night air lifted the light edge of her dress in the deft way of breezeghosts and cryptbreaths.

Hello, she said, not aloud. Understanding that dog and man were Presences, Bunny felt no less shy about her old body's crags and collapsing cliffs.

She could hear the Helltel's reluctant elevator struggling to lift The Mister and the three guests.

3.

Acker was the one who got us into calling the spirits "Presences." We called them "ghosts" before that, and, a long time ago, everyone called them "haints."

You couldn't easily tell when someone in the consignment-bar was a Presence.

When a stranger came in, we gave each other signals: we rocked our heads the way you would to a little music, and that meant it was a real person; we nodded slowly up and down, a mild warning, and that meant it was a Presence. Occasionally one of us nodded at the same time the other person rocked. The ceremony could be confusing.

An animal or plant could be a Presence, though when that happened—and that did happen—we would rock-nod-guffaw-gasp and give up and try again. A consignment item could be a Presence for which we felt custodial responsibility.

A lined jacket slips alone into a consignment-bar and, sits, sighs, desleeves, drifts four empty arms onto the bar. "What'll you have, Miss?" the bartender asks.

That is not a joke. Is it?

Acker, too, could be confusing. Thirty or so, or fifty or sixty or so, or undefinably epochal, she had a punk thing going from the white face makeup to the blue lipstick (black sometimes) to the white fingernails to the bright white boots so bright you could not really see her feet. And that—the blurring of her feet—is, perhaps, why she seemed without weight.

She wore white kid gloves. Tattoos of slender tree stems, cardinal red, reached all the way down her arms and all the way up her snow-white legs into the crotch-high blue jean cutoffs she wore in the summer and autumn and early fall, and wore over web-glimmering white leggings in winter.

She was lifelike. Her tattoos were lifelike. We knew it was thrilling for young Woolman to see those shrieking fire-red stems reaching toward Acker's thighs.

"Realistic, am I right?" she said to Woolman the very first time she caught his gaze.

We were sure looking. All of us accepted Acker's invitation to look at her newest piercings and tattoos.

We had seen Woolman's best friend, Lincoln Lennox, looking at her like that, looking and looking.

Her arms and legs were slender but bodybuilder-strong, which mattered. Her muscularity was not more important to Woolman and Lincoln than the wonder of, the beauty of, her altered flesh and skin. On the wooden floor of the consignment-bar and beyond, she cast unusually agile shadows—you felt they could leap into you.

Our community in North Carolina was not at all where Acker belonged, but at certain times revenants like her did appear out of nowhere, did grow here, became regulars and not and regulars once more.

Her exposed belly button, circled by the tattoo words, *Discuss Rules Beforehand,* was pierced with a metal tuning fork embossed with the ratio 3:2. Tiny but real, the thing could be struck and sounded, a severe-true-serene tone.

She had platinum-roots white hair. Most of the time it was a high, pale wave cresting above her forehead. She had a sewn-on pouch—it had been made to look like an alert erection—just under her jeans zipper, and if she wanted to yank your chain she called her codpiece "Little Mike," petted him, and said things like "Little Mike likes," "Little Mike listens," "Say it into Little Mike." Mike was a fake microphone, probably fake, but she and Mike's companion, Siri, could make you believe otherwise.

She wore men's cologne splashed all over her arms and face, and she refreshed it throughout the day, and that was (maybe) a good thing because she vaped—more or less nonstop—a certain kind of marijuana formula she called Prom. She had a constant cloud of what looked like steam around her when she was mouthing the silver vapetube the size of an old-school cigar tube. *Vwew.* Softly. *Vwew.* That was the sound her delivery system made. An aura came from her that was strong enough to alter you.

We believed she was realalien. We speculated that she was alienreal, a person who had crossed through all our naming systems, had left herself at the places she lived and died, and had brought some of her dead self and some of her living self to Cord. She knew where The Passages were, the standing-on-the-ground places and the feet-in-the-river and the butt-on-the-treebranch places, where one could be found by the entering or departing Presences. When she arrived here in 2008, she said she already knew.

Right in front of customers, the regs and the nonregs, too, she lifted her skinny, muscular arms, and kept them up in the air, and trembled from holding them up so long. She said this posture was a yoga thing, for which she had a name, BDSM. "Explain, Siri," Acker would ask her iPhone, and Siri would answer, "Lifestyle of the bitch and infamous," or would answer, "Touring …touring …" while her humachine mind engine-searched humankind's coughing language-faucets.

4.

On the day of Lincoln Lennox's lynching, November 8, 2016, investigators came to look at the swing set where his mother found him at 2 a.m.

Cord, at this time of year, was holding the first meetings to prepare to host the Eleventh Annual Soldier's Joy Festival, the big community music festival held March 31st to April 6th in memory of two Iraq-occupation Army personnel who died together in the same drowning incident in Ephesus Swamp two days after they returned home from Iraq. Private First Class Edward "Eddie" Carter Lang, age twenty-eight. Specialist Aaeedah Willerton Clodd, age twenty-nine; everyone called her Eedie. They had been friends of Junior Stanley in the time before he had become what he called a Proud Home Guard Boy. He and other members of the Proud Boys club and the Prayer Patriots club were the chief organizers of the weeklong Soldier's Joy celebrations, their tribute to the two young heroes—"heroes" is the word we feel we should use and, with confused respect, should promote—who had been told the cause was just and had, like us, been convinced.

The investigators came to Stanley's~~Acker's~~ Stanley's because two belts had served for the lynching, and the belts still had the green $ consignment tags. (That specific $ sign meant the belts were Stanley's item. Green meant the purchase price was negotiable.)

"The Swing Playground" is how people refer to this playground at Dowless Place Trailer Park. There was no bench or chair from which Lincoln might have launched. No bench or chair markings on the ground. It seemed he stepped off the swing attached to the spar.

His feet were six inches from the dirt.

If you're from this region in the South, you know all these details matter, because an amateur hanging—too long a fall—can separate the head from the body, flinging them in opposite directions; and the hanging man's toes touching dirt—striking or spiking into the ground—can leave the dead eyes open and staring down, the mouth in rictus.

Mrs. Jadia Lennox, his mother, said the shoes on Lincoln were not his and the two belts were not his and Lincoln had already discovered other ways to get out of here than tearing his mother's heart out by killing himself, and she said Cord was a small community and everyone—everyone and not just some—knew she was telling the truth, that he had been killed, that he had been lynched.

Woolman, Lincoln's closest friend, pleaded with Jadia to avoid touching her son's face, his hands and feet. Acker joined Woolman in the van to which Lincoln's football coach carried the body, the buckled loop still tight around Lincoln's neck, the whole belt-noose trailing. Ignoring the coach's reminder that the coroner was on the way, Jadia touched his hair to neaten it, she kissed his swollen hands, she made Woolman agree, Acker agree: "Lincoln didn't kill hisself. He never would."

"He didn't," they said. "Never."

Acker did not touch his hands, though she loved his hands and strong fingers. She did not kissbite the edges of his ears as she had at other times, but found herself looking at Woolman whose stultified body was like a clock laid facedown.

Acker would not lift Jadia away from Lincoln. That she felt in this moment she could, could lift Jadia and Lincoln and Woolman and van and Cord and motherfuckingcountry over her head and onto her shoulders, reminded her how the levers and pulleys of syntax fail famous writers.

In the way Lincoln would revoice something his mother repeatedly said, Jadia said for him, "Sorrymomsorry—sorrymomsorry—sorrymomsorry—" trying to bring him to life five syllables at a time, the world intruding through the van windows, the restive sense and bright sound of him gone, the intense beam.

Minister Stanley took Lincoln's death hard. He was a man of God, and you could see God helped him recognize what people with no honest faith at all could plainly know about the place we live, about this refuge of the aggrieved entitled white wannabe Neo-Nazis of Unite the Right and the followers of the evangelical gospel of the Word of Faith. Months after Lincoln died, that boy Dylann Roof who killed so many in the AME church in Charleston, South Carolina, was on his way to seek succor in Cord before he was arrested in Shelby. At one time or another, plenty of the Trumpwaffen thugs came to drink at this pool of tears. Everyone in Cord understood. Minister Stanley understood. To not say it aloud was destroying Minister Stanley inside.

Three agents came to investigate the lynching. Two of the agents made a quick trip in, a quick trip out. One of them was a looked-like-she-was-just-out-of-high-school woman agent; apparently her job was to take pictures of the site, of Lincoln in the morgue, and to take candid pictures of his family members and friends as—what?—suspects?

The agent who appeared to be her closest partner, not much older, a boyfriend we thought, asked vague questions that were related to Lincoln's character and behavior, to his habits, his recent moods and actions. The agent had no curiosity about the manner and mission of Lincoln's killer or killers.

They asked for the name of Lincoln's father. Told by Minister that Lovel Lennox had died in the war, they did not ask when or ask which one of the many possible wars. When Minister added, "He's hereabouts," they only noted vaguely the two words as something they imagined he might have said.

The third agent, keeping his distance from the other two, stayed in town in the Helltel: an old-man agent, a Black man, panther dark. He was friends right off with Webb the bar dog who was more talkative than most dogs and, come to think of it, than most of us.

The old-man agent asked everyone questions, and it was clear he was never going to stop thinking of new questions to ask. He asked the townspeople questions, and he even asked the young people who were on the West Cord Knights football team to tell about their teammate Lincoln, to explain why he would have suicided just before a big game that everyone knew mattered intensely to him, why he would have suicided at a playground more or less in his own family's backyard.

We talked to this panther. We told him the facts we could think to tell. There was an unholy triangle of Lincoln and Acker and Woolman, and Jadia didn't like it but couldn't interfere, and didn't understand, not at all, and she wanted to know if anyone had a Black teenage son who didn't fear for him. "Our best receiver," the coach said at the memorial service, and offered, "Lincoln was a reader, a nerdish one like no boy I met ever. He'd rather go into a book or into space than onto the field. But he went on the field. Lincoln went on the field."

He took cornet lessons from Mack Metzanteen Watson, sometimes practicing in the consignment-bar where no one would speak the truth about Mack's—how to put this?—long record of inadequacy as a teacher. Lincoln was a mama's boy, everyone knew. His mother pulled for that boy like a tree pulls light. Her Lincoln was an intelligent, sensitive young man. Why would he suicide on a swing set where the first to find him hanging might be children?

Since everyone agreed that Woolman was his best friend, the old agent asked who had questioned Woolman.

No one, we said.

And Lincoln's girlfriend?

No one.

We explained that Acker was girlfriend to them both, and that arrangement was no problem for the three of them, really no problem. We agreed with him that the district attorney or someone, surely someone, needed to depose Miss Acker, which was not done even when she herself insisted she be questioned.

"The local police—they've questioned suspects?"

We have no local police in Cord. We have police support from other jurisdictions. We have two retired estate lawyers, who keep to themselves unless buying fair catch old properties. We have reporters of different kinds but none full-time. Had a radio station once that broadcast from the back room in the hardware store. Only have the tower now. The room in the back—the word *Historical* on a clouded-over copper plate on the door—is where you can find an enormous evidence stockpile of voter fraud activities that would invalidate the past twenty-four years of elections. The North Carolina state motto—isn't it?—is "To seem to be, rather than to be."

The story lasted five days in the North Carolina papers; a reporter, L.G. Hearn, came here for *The Guardian*. All the way from England. And for a while, we thought his reporting might produce a more wide-ranging set of questions. And for a while, we thought Mr. Hearn might follow up, that he might put other reporters on the scent, since he had confidently determined it was "a suspected lynching."

Nothing followed.

Isn't Hearn a good name for a coward? If you were writing a book, it would serve.

Anyway, how would one reporter matter? The right-wing Civitas Institute has controlled most of the print news in this part of the country since 2001. And a long time before that, though with a gentler hand once.

By Thanksgiving, the district attorney called the whole matter of Lincoln Lennox's death "settled." Not a single editor or reporter for the county newspapers disagreed. Not a single eastern or coastal North Carolina radio or television station investigated further. Not one local official or state legislator took increased interest in the case of the lynching of Lincoln Lennox.

The wrinkles at the temples of the old agent were bluish-black zigzag marks. A high forehead, and a hairline shaved down to black stubble. We were, of course, surprised to see the machetes swinging in saddle-weight black leather scabbards at his skinny hips. This has always been true: into the story of Cord enters the searcher for the wonderful, a panther, an old drummer, a pirate, a tinman thief; they find something here that extinguishes reason, that relieves suffering while releasing new suffering. And that story will not leave.

We nodded at him. We rocked at him. Doubting nods, rocks. A Presence? A person? Sometimes when we looked at him we thought, *He's right here*. Sometimes we thought, *He's over there*.

The coroner, Mr. Bergermeadow, a man whose history is our history, a white man with white underneath his skin and way down under it, the Black of Black ancestors, offered his own explanation on live television. He said, "You have to understand, suicide with these people is common as measles" and "These people off themselves all the time. They do." He said, "They are statistics," which he meant to say but then earnestly meant us to hear, "There are statistics." He repeatedly said, "There are statistics, there are statistics," as if colluding with all mad tea-party listeners in a pledge to erase the unreal real.

Mr. Bergermeadow is so like our president that whenever he is outright lying he has the identical eye-squint pig-snort tell.

Mr. Bergermeadow, his name offal you can lie down in and consume, pronounced his report was concluded. When a reporter for the *Atlanta Constitution Times* asked how soon the public would have access to the report, he said, "These people ... deserve our prayers. These people, you have to understand ..."

When one of these people, Jadia Lincoln, found her son, she saw his scratched-up face and his beaten-in cheeks and chin and nose, she saw the knot on his forehead. When the belts were removed, the scar on his neck was green "like some mold or something been on it," she said. Rope-scar marked his wrists and ankles though no rope bound them that way when she pulled him from the swing set in an adrenaline rush of strength so powerful she could have snapped the whole contraption apart. And as for his neck bruise, wasn't that the result of leather belts bigger than and wider than normal and not new at all, and shouldn't the belts be taken somewhere for forensic testing, and where was his favorite red cap?

You think Jadia would not have fixed so much attention on the belts, on the cap? If you think that, you don't live in Cord where so many of the injured dead refuse to stay invisible.

Lincoln's wounds were indicated on the coroner's report as being consistent with "ant injuries."

Jadia said there were no ants. *There were no ants.* That lie—the ant injury shit meant for stupid people to go along with—was an insult to her, meant specifically to insult her intelligence and the intelligence of all her own people and of all "these people" in our country. *There were no ants. There were no ants. There were no goddamn ants.*

5.

Some folks went into hiding for a few hours after two of the three investigators left, but in a little while the usual silver holiday tinsel and fiberglass cherubs and the *Celebrate Cord!!!* Christmas decorations were strung up across the central two blocks of our town of twenty-one hundred people. The Soldier's Joy festivities in March would include more red tinsel added to the silver, and hundreds more of the winged gungoyles with goyledickguns in hand. The festival, which was always well attended by Cordites and by people from as far away as the Outer Banks, did not draw visitors back here for the Christmas season.

Minister Stanley and Junior Stanley and Woolman and the dog Webb were in the consignment-bar, telling the old machete-wearing agent about the festival four months away, asking whether he planned to stay that long.

Minister described the two weeks of early evening fiddle and banjo and singing performances that would take place in March; he said he and Junior would introduce him to festivalgoers. "You'll see," Minister said, "this thing is unreal, it's—you know what I mean—"

"Off the rails," said Minister's son Stanley Junior.

Minister's enthusiasm for the endless covers of the classic tune "Soldier's Joy," reminded us that his dead teenage daughter Lisbet had been a promising Cord guitarist and fiddle player and singer. She had absorbed the sounds of everything and everyone around her. Minister and Junior had once used the same words, "unreal" and "off the rails," to describe her, and they found secret comfort in the remembering echo the words made now.

Lisbet was a clever creature, and she picked up our impulses and intentions, the giving and withholding voices in our heads and the ones in our guts. A flowering person like Lisbet causes vigilance in the old; your instinct is to guard her spathes of fire.

Stanley Junior explained to the old agent, "My sister—she's around, if you look. I mean, the pictures."

The agent had not, in fact, become alert to the pictures since they always moved. The picture of Lisbet, chin on fiddle, big-brimmed straw hat kind of floating on her head because of holding all her hair: that one would be to the right of the doorframe between the bar and the consignment, and the next day it would be on the left, or it would be upside down or on the ceiling and reflecting your bald spot. The picture of Lisbet with her daddy, Minister Stanley, both their eyes dreamily closed, mouths open, their coppery faces identically pushed forward in concentrated singing: one day the picture would be where it belonged, in the Musical bin of the consignment, and the next day, unframed in the Papers Good bin. There was infectious amnesia about that bin sign, which Minister and Acker and Junior had crossed through and spelled right, "Paper Goods," and which would then return to its natural wrong spelling and cause one of us to ask if the sign hadn't been corrected, and cause all of us to say, Well, maybe not. When he was still with us, Lincoln liked to prank us by moving the pictures of Lisbet, but he knew and we knew other forces were also involved.

Minister Stanley said, "She was a mischievous girl, praise God."

The agent joined no one in praising God or saying amen. For a lot of hours every day during late November and December he parked himself in one of the two bar booths more or less at the entrance to the john. He hunched down, moving only barely in his loose clothes, a booth-creature. Sometimes he brought with him a bag, an actual blue plastic garbage bag in the shape of a spider sac. He would

20

open it to show you. Clothes. Not his. Not clothes for consignment. Young people's clothes.

Once, Acker asked, "WTF?" and the old man patted the bogey-thing, and said, "No introductions needed," as if that could possibly be true.

We gave the old-man agent the name Mr. Panther. He had a real name, and we really did not care.

No one was in the consignment shop, so Acker let Woolman follow her to the bar. She had a new specimen in hand. The creature had been brought in by the skinhead delivery driver for Cheese Head deli products. Junior and Minister called him Brother Head for no good reason and, because that made him smile, they eventually called him Brother H. We were pretty sure that all of his clothes, down to his shackle-buckle boots and wide belts, were from our consignment. He came across as a gentle creature, a son of Stone Mountain, Georgia, a failure-to-launch launched alone into a story not at all his own. He came across as a swineherd or a tinker in a playful, disturbing old Appalachian tale. He came across as the small, clenched fist of a boynazi convinced that under the right conditions he could cast a giant, crushing shadow. He came across as something pathetic and pathological we had conjured more or less intentionally.

Acker removed the twelve bricks stacked in a Jenga pattern on top of The Book's place of honor. Our tradition, which was as old as the bar, sixty-some years, was to place the specimens in their envelopes inside this hardback 722-page monster poetry anthology, *The Silence That Is Within Us*, edited by a Mr. Rodney Swan Jones. Consignment-bar regulars like Brother H and sometimes even well-informed strangers brought the butterflies in from our mountains and woods, and if the creatures needed to be euthanized and opened out and arranged, that was done. The wax-paper envelope was marked, and the thing was tucked in a space remaining in the crowded Book, and The Book was shut and everything pressed down again under the bricks.

This ritual made sense to you if you were a local and knew Minister Stanley, a funny, odd man, a man with religion. He called it Old Religion, not wishing for it to be mistakenly associated with the Prosperity Gospel or the Word of Faith people, a cult that traveled through scam Christian healing missionaries from our region to other mutant Christian ministries in Portugal, and returned here in a rabid form quickly infecting hundreds, draining its followers— many of them were undocumented immigrants easily exploited—of all resources, hiring them out as laborers that they could continually extort in Christ's name.

Minister Stanley and his son Junior were Mixed Race. You have to put a name on that; around here you have to put a name on that. A dark race of Black mixed with a lighter brown race—not a lucky combination. Minister Stanley's religion had no actual name, as far as anyone knew, though he'd told us he had been Methodist once, once Presbyter, once Baptist, once Catholic, once Episcopalian, once Universalist; he was of Mixed Religion, you'd have to say. He was dark copper, had silvery brows and silvery five o'clock shadow on the copper skin of his face, wore silver-rimmed glasses with mirrory lenses, a silvery, coppery fellow except for dark-edged, golden age spots at his temples and cheeks and the base of his throat, and on his hands.

According to him, The Book, *The Silence That Is Within Us,* came to the bar with Old Drummer, a Presence, probably—maybe—no, probably—who bartered The Book and two large jugs of her home-brewed moonshine for three cloth coats of three different sizes and weights so OD could put on layers and peel them off according to the season. She'd said she planned to move to the Piedmont from her home in the Pisgah Wilderness near Brevard. Maybe she did, how could we know? She was deep fog, Minister Stanley said. It was understood that she really was. When you looked into the folds in the thin pine woods where the moon and the wind in the trees danced brindled, prowling shadows through the mist and you thought she was absent there, you felt she was present. When you knew she was present and standing in front of you, you felt she was totally absent. She called herself Old OD, unconcerned about being twice old. "Old OD's here to bargain," she would say, and "Old OD's got a proposition for you." Never used the word "I," ever.

The bricks keeping The Book pressed closed were the blackened bricks of The Pleasant Hill Missionary Baptist Church that burned down in East Howellsville in Reagan's time, one of four torched African-American churches within sixty miles of our town. Plenty of reminders here in Cord and all around us of interleaving losses.

Acker placed the new specimen. She lifted out another, much older. "You've got to see this." The butterfly had come in from Union Vedder, the oldest of the regulars at the bar.

Explaining Union Vedder is going to be a twisty operation, no getting around that. Union had died in the spring of 1781 when his detachment was chasing Cornwallis from the interior of the Carolinas to Wilmington; years later he died again on Cape Fear in 1865; and one hundred and forty years later he died again from a self-inflicted accidental gunshot—that was in 2005; people still talk about his death because of running debate about whether you should say "self-inflicted accidental gunshot" or "accidental self-inflicted gunshot."

He stuck around, you could tell, because the cash register would pop open by itself, and everyone would remember Union's warning never to tempt a "convicted robber" like him. Well, that was the joke people made about Union, who took a postage stamp out of the cash register one time—only one time—1958, when the bar and consignment was called simply Stanley's—and never lived that down because of how the locals hounded him about "the robbery." "You keep that cash drawer closed tight or you'll make me a rich man," he had always said, because, by his own definition, he had a good sense of humor. He was certainly a Presence.

Union was and is a learned man and well-read and thoughtful. He free-roamed Cord and beyond Cord and far beyond. If, as most folks did, you let Union in, you knew he would travel further into your private business than you yourself had likely ever traveled.

He was opinionated, that was obvious. Inscrutable: obvious.

You could call Union Vedder our diviner.

For about two hundred and twenty years, our farmers and thread mill laborers and educators and the like brought Union our own tales and brought him secondhand and thirdhand tales, and some tales that were not our own.

We let him in.

Knowing he liked the weird stories best, folks would stink them up for him, put some eerie in the brew. Preferring our stories over his, Union rarely included himself in the retellings.

To be clear: after his death in 1781, he was a spirit and not alive in the flesh but present among us until 1866; from 1867 to 1961, he was a spirit and actually alive here in the flesh; from 1962 to 2005, he was, well, we couldn't tell.

We knew he died—re-died—in 2005. He would have wanted his memorial urn to say

ACCIDENTAL
SELF-INFLICTED

No one seems sure about the resting place of his ashes or when he was ashed. His death, this particular death of his, occurring one day after the solemn ceremonies for Private First Class Eddie Lang and Specialist Eedie Clodd, was, needless to say, thought to be insignificant. Some deaths are rightly described as untimely. This one was poorly timed.

From 2006 to the present day—this is lookinglassy for sure—Union has been alive here in spirit but not in the actual flesh. If anyone can put to words Cord's weird story it is Union Vedder—he himself would tell you that, canmightprobably tell you that, willpossiblywill tell you that, maybe.

Acker pulled out the wax-paper envelope containing the butterfly that had been brought there before Brother H's butterfly. She showed us. She said, "Add me foursevens," something she said—like so many things she said—that did not add up, though tonally it resembled "Riddle me this." She read the location and name: "Page 718, the poet, David Lawson." Something about the way she read, always made you think the poet's name was the real name of the butterfly, like, *Polygonia Comma Davidlawson nymphalidae.*

She read the David Lawson poem, and before she finished the end, *"and belched the national anthem, / and told the cops she never saw him sober,"* the beer mugs were raised. If the thing was a good poem the mugs were raised. A middling-poor poem, mugs raised. A barking doggerel, mugs raised.

Minister Stanley used to be chief reader of the butterfly information and the poems, but he came to prefer Acker's readings; when she read, her voice crackled and bristled like iced-over spruce trees will do. She gave a better ceremony. She was, she said so herself, a performer. She came here from New York where—she wanted us to know—she had been "fuckin major," "a fuckin critical fuckin success," and no one's creation but her own.

She was a writer of some kind and probably actually famous at one time or another—how were we supposed to know—but she said "they" set out to kill her in London, England, and they set out to kill her in Reichskirche, Germany, and they set out to kill her in the Village in New York, and so she went to Japan to learn Okuni dancing, a kind of goth-liturgical-stripper-disco dancing she had mistakenly thought might lead to a career at a shrine somewhere.

When no shrine would have her, she came here to be "an owner of something for once" and own and lose the consignment-bar, all in one year, '08 to '09. She lived in the Helltel, where she took her place as "the headliner in this fucked-over 8-track-porn swamptown." Her version of her story, that's what we have.

In front of the others, she took Woolman's hands up and caressed them and pressed the back of them into the center of her flimsy T-shirt upon which she had Sharpied the words, Rock Abrasian Tool. The same way she would do with Lincoln, she pressed the center of herself to his center. She raised her arms at her sides, trembled a little, raised them above her head. Woolman was seventeen, the same age as Lincoln Lennox had been. Woolman was an excitable young man, and he didn't take his hands away exactly at the moment that she let go.

"Woman," she said, "don't romance me when I'm giving you some."

His name, Woolman Edwards, didn't matter to him so much that he wanted to argue with her about her renaming him Woman. And he didn't mind about her telling anyone who would listen that she had "two boys grinding my coffee."

There was about twenty-five years (or, depending on your perspective, forty-five years, or four hundred and ten) of age difference between Lincoln and Acker, between Woolman and Acker. Cordites talked about that kind of thing. Hunched over the three hundred twenty-nine million piece puzzle of us, people talk, endlessly fitting the wrong piece in the wrong place. Why would she take up with two high school students at the same time? And why flaunt them like some kind of hetero-lesbian-pedophile-miscegenator?

She and Woolman walked back through the bar into the consignment shop. On principle, our townspeople do not like to recycle. They do like to recycle for money, and so do the other people moving through, and so do the presences from Decker to Ninepin and way up the road and stretching past and beyond. You could buy here every kind of Assorted item: Assorted Men, Assorted Children, Assorted Home, Assorted Recreation, Assorted Religious, Assorted Miscellaneous, Assorted Women, including Women Intimates and Women Wares and Women Special Needs, Assorted Papers Good, and Musical. You could buy dolls of every kind and the special Mrs. Labboard methdolls, too. You could buy paper fans, the porch and church and political campaign kinds. Acker herself had a fan with a penmanship lesson on one side and palmistry on the other: it had come in from Tina Titter Thillisthom, who, in all negotiations over consignment goods, roar-scowled at you and shriek-giggled at herself if she succeeded in making you feel small.

One whole bin was for gloves, men's and women's. One bin marked "Best Offer" held neatly nested ball caps, hundreds: ACLU and MAMA and FEEL THE BERN? and BULL! and a curious form of MAGA hat with a WRRWUW overpatch—a lot of them. You could buy scroll paintings—the truth, scroll paintings—including seven of the ten famous White Stone Scrolls, famous here anyway, and underworldly, and, okay, overpriced like obseemly items are sometimes. They were painted by James Harris Jr., a local Presence who appeared in Cord from Jasper, Texas, in 1999. Consigned us his scrolls, brought in a slightly damaged Phoebis Sennae Fredchappell Pieridae from his car grille, drank a beer or two, tried on a pageant crown, and approved of the Chappell poem (a Fredifying verse, with "blind whirlpool galaxies" and "marauding stars" and "mad inventories"). We've never sold one of the scrolls, but how does that matter since we never see Mr. Harris? He's here, we figure, but we never see him.

The largest clothing rack was the muumuu rack. The muumuus were popular items never out of style. Near that rack was a wall shelf of bewigged, featureless, rounded pine posts. The Pines, a large family of thirteen, had identical long necks, and they shared among them one warped five-by-eight unvarnished lumber shoulder. The wigs The Pines wore, all different kinds, were askew—"adjusted" is the better word—because of Junior Stanley's ongoing attempts to position them in such a way as to have the dissociated family members show each other some regard.

You could buy heavily used and hardly worn wigs, shirts, pants, hats, shoes, jackets, fleeces, socks, socklets, and coats and muumuus and every other kind of item before you went into the bar where you would, of course, model. The bar, over-air-conditioned in summer and underheated the rest of the year, was not warm ever, so you would model a jaunty hat, a bathrobe, a wrestling singlet, a silk gown, coat, whatnot, and leave it on, and have a drink, and Acker or Minister Stanley would read your tag, and Junior Stanley would read your tag, and Minister and Junior would argue about the price (Junior always wanted to go higher; Minister preferred practically giving things away, but not utterly away like Acker), and the item would go on your bar tab.

6.

Minister Stanley and Webb nodded at the stranger appearing in the bar as if from nowhere, a worn-looking and unkempt guy modeling a stiff wool vest, nut brown, that was too youngish and too small for him and too much like something from another century. The green tag hung from the underarm seam. Minister said, "Seven dollar," and, not in the mood to argue, glared at Junior who thought nine or ten was better. Handing the stranger the beer he had ordered, Minister said, "Total eleven dollar."

The stranger couldn't translate, you could see.

"Want to keep a tab?" Minister asked. To help him, he said, "One-stop shop," but that befuddled the stranger more.

The stranger said, "I have been away a long time," and he seemed to be talking through a deep tunnel of amazement directly toward young Woolman.

"I'm home now," said the stranger.

"You look good in it," said Woolman, trying to sell. Selling was in his job description at Stanley's~~Acker's~~Stanley's, and he was serious about his obligations.

You might think Woolman would have recognized the longtime traveller.

He didn't. We didn't.

Almost did.

Didn't.

Minister Stanley slowly nodded at the stranger, Acker nodded a little more slowly as if the story of this moment was one she recognized. Junior Stanley rocked his head but it turned into a nod toward The Pines.

"That handsome clothing item makes you look expensive," said Acker. She asked her codpiece, "Mike—you like?"

Mike clicked twice, which made Siri say, "He likes."

"It lends dignity," said Minister Stanley lying, lying perfectly. Isn't this as true here as anywhere on this earth: when the word of God is sufficiently deformed, it is a money-making blessing for anyone who goes into business or politics.

"I've been so thirsty," said the stranger. He seemed to know us, the place, The Pines. We-it-they seemed to know him. "This is weird. I knew this would be weird, but I didn't know how much. I walked around the place a few times before I walked in, because I understood this would be—you know—upsetting. For me. And for you, too."

"Yeah. It can get weird here," said Woolman. He strode closer to the traveller, his attention on the pattern in the wool material of the vest: upturned trumpets or upturned trumpet-shape blossoms in gold- and amber-colored thread. Woolman was not a touchy young person as far as any of us could tell, yet he touched the vest on the man, looked at the consignment label. He stepped back to discern what he had touched.

"Collector's item," said Minister, a trustmasked man not to be trusted.

The stranger drew Woolman's gaze to him. He asked, "You can't see who I am. I—understandable, of course you can't, how could—" He held his arms up because he was on the way to claiming a hug. He put them down but he did not step away from Woolman, who stood very close and did not back off, who once more touched the vest in a way you'd never see him do at any other time.

Woolman said, "Oh."

He worked the vest tag between his thumb and his other fingers. He looked longer into the man's face. He said, "Oh."

He almost collapsed there and then.

Acker caught Woolman in her arms.

7.

Woolman, Jacob's son, had been five years old when Jacob left him and his mother Marie. It wasn't exactly Lincoln's death that brought Jacob I. Edwards back to his hometown of Cord where people will notice you are missing but will figure you are not actually far away. No one knew Jacob had been alone in the woods near Lake Michaux, only thirty-eight miles from Cord. From November 2004 to 2016, Jacob lived completely alone and often starving in his falling-down hovel near the lake that poisoned him each time he drank from it.

On the ninth of November, Lincoln visited and walked near Jacob in the densest part of the woods where flashing blades of early-morning sunlight struck edge against edge.

The glimmering figure resolving into a young Black man, disappeared, his voice soughing: "Don't know how I came here."

He reappeared but with bright sparking fires at his feet and hands and throat and head.

He disappeared as if inside his rustled words: "How did I come here, Jacob?"

Reaching for the young man, trying to hold him, hear him a moment longer, Jacob decided he must return to Cord.

8.

Lincoln's death caused the machete-carrying Mr. Panther to move here in December. It brought him here, that's true, but what made the old agent stay?

When a man with machetes moves to Cord, Cord hawkgurgles awake to see. He hauled three large pieces of luggage from the back and front seats of his VW Bug, the green color of a tomato hornworm. He arranged for a month's rent at the Helltel and, on his very first day and every day at sunrise, he walked west up Sweet Thorn Road to the playground where there were eight sets of swings. He tipped up the little basket swings for toddlers and he gave a push to the other swings, didn't miss one, touched every empty swing. Could be that no one was in the black rubber seats. Could be every seat was occupied, and could be that someone moved with him from swing to swing, and asked to be rocked or sailed up. We saw him do this because we could not miss seeing those swing sets. Not anymore.

He walked a quarter of a mile up the same side of Sweet Thorn to an expanse of slash pines where there was an old wooden marker with a command carved in: Walk. We could tell that Mr. Panther intuited how the transfiguring hours among young trees and decaying tree ancestors are not the same as other hours. He knew the way in. He knew the way out.

We wanted to ask, "You from around this area, Mr. Panther?" and we could ask since he came to the consignment-bar every afternoon all through November, drank beer but not too much, hunted through Assorted Miscellaneous, Teen, Pre-teen, and Religious and Old Farm. He bought two WRRUWW hats and put them in his blue plastic bag.

He lifted off the bricks and paged through The Book, and far in, far into The Book where more than the incandescent dust of butterfly bodies was pressed. The man liked poetry, we guessed: one of that kind who liked phrases to lose in the pulse-thrilling fight with clauses.

He gave Acker's slender tattooed legs his passing attention, looked in at us, prying, liking us no less.

He returned to those swings, returned to Ephesus Swamp. He made a routine of driving his little Bug to the crossing arm for the train; with the engine running, he watched the speeding train, which has no exact physical form for us in Cord because we know the menacing, marvelous thing by the echoing warning-alarm sounds. Without exception, he stood there at the crossing, arms at his sides, counting the railroad ties in both directions, or marking time according to a secret system or plan.

We could have asked him plenty of questions, but we didn't know how.

By early February, he was always accompanied by a mockingbird who had come out of the woods with him and had not returned to them. She established territory at the margins of the Helltel's ruined apple orchard in the back where they could take off for a sunset stroll together, and where she could harass squirrels and other critters of ground and sky. They enjoyed each other's company in the late evening when he sat out in a rocker, a headlamp on, a notebook in his lap, her reading over his shoulder sometimes or sometimes affectionately perching on his knee and showing him her pretty self, or asking him a sipwhistling unsonglike question that would ruin his sleep or cast a deep sleeping spell over him. She climbed down and back up his long machetes, rubbing herself against them, hoarsely whispering.

After their adventures in Ephesus Swamp, he often took her whole body in his hands, like a pigeon keeper will do, and he stroked the pinfeathers on her neck and face, and let his fingers appreciate her talons.

We called her Mrs. Panther. Each clever nomenclator at Stanley's Acker'sStanley's claimed to have originated the name.

Some of us knew she was Lisbet Pluchet Stanley. If your people six generations ago knew about the one Michaux-Pluchet descendent who fled Highlands, North Carolina, to hide out in this part of the Piedmont, then your people knew about the one Pluchet descendent who had married into the Stanley family, and that particle of information was your clue about Lisbet.

Before becoming a mockingbird, Lisbet had been our talented small fish in the Appalachian pool here teeming with fishes of extraordinary appeal. She died at a young age. Died but never left the place where, sooner or later, there would have been nothing for her. She became a Presence and knew the way to and from The Passages and could seduce you fast as a preacher in an expensive car and fine suit—we all knew this from the ghost stories that are the lost-in-the-swamp versions. Did Mr. Panther know this?

Well, he must not have. She could be the devil you had desired all your life. She could teach you to devil like you'd never done or even thought to do.

Could her parents and her brother Junior Stanley ever believe she perdured?

She was Minister Stanley's and Orelia Jones-Stanley's other child; they had Junior but he was not enough—even he understood that eventually—and she was the natural favorite at her birth, at that very instant.

On the day after Lisbet's wake Minister and Orelia did as everyone had long expected. They left each other. Left each other, stayed in Cord, never passed a week without a visit or a phone call or a shared meal or a wash day or a stayover. They grew old apart and together and apart: nothing out of the ordinary for a separated couple to be in compromised conviviality that eventually results in a freakishly beautiful human bolus, the way a tree ringed in barbwire fencing absorbs the wire completely.

Cord watches.

The citizens of Cord don't miss a thing because we are of one conflicted mind, and we are always minding.

Mr. Panther put the headlamp on every evening at sunset. He sat outside, staring at the slash pines bordering the swamp twenty yards beyond the Helltel's wrecked apple orchard. His cone of light almost seemed to reach inside and search that nearby section of swamp, where in certain places, decimus bushes were so densely clustered only clearing would make walking possible. He slashed away at the bushes. We should have, could have asked whether there was something about that particular bush that he should tell us.

Mrs. Panther flew into and out of his lamplight, sang mournfully, and fell silent while he clouted and slashed and moved aside decimus branches like a man answering to legions of haints.

9.

February 29 at 2 a.m. illuminated drapes of restless, twisting bright air kicked up and out, reflecting their light on our windows. The dancing fire, easy to mistake at first for the pyrotorsions of sunrise flaring inside circling fog, appeared on the town square at the intersection of the Perfection Lumber store and Cord Town Hall & Museum and Mrs. Chambers' Grocery & Deli and Stanley'sAcker'sStanley's.

Normal size but made of green wood hewn roughly, jointed together in a hurry. A thick rope, like boat-docking rope, hung from the crossbeam. A hangman's noose. Gray sneakers attached by the shoelaces to the noose. The whole thing burning, persistently flaming up and flaming out, smoking more than burning, smoke downbranching, live cinder-eyes in the slender lengthening arms and stems, live sparking stars inside the eyes.

Webb and Mrs. Panther barked and shrieked Mr. Panther awake in order to bring him, to show him. They brought Minister Stanley and Stanley Junior and Acker and Woolman to the site where the odd creation was collapsing.

Union Vedder, the first there, of course, quietly, unobtrusively stood among them. He scratched Webb's thick neck and his dog brows. Union lifted his own neck, offered his head to Mrs. Panther, who liked flying through and back through his face and his sparse, stringy hair, as bracing for her as needling through an icy waterfall. You might imagine discomfort for Union; it was not that. To be threaded, to be worn and wormed, to become thinner cloth and rag and tissue and air—to be the void who can rise so lightly from your bed is not so bad.

The crosslight of the moon and the fracturing swingfire. The sighing of the flames. The acrid scent of the burning sneakers and of the accelerant used to ignite them. The bloodrust airtaste of the doused, excited, heavy rope. So many years after his many deaths, it nevertheless startled Union how easily he became the passing things before him, how he could be Time observing time.

"Jesusfuck," said Acker, who recognized the sneakers as Lincoln's, the ones Lincoln was actually wearing on the day he died, not the too-small ones forced onto his feet when he was executed. Woolman, held lightly but closely by Acker like she would do when she would gather both Woolman and Lincoln into her arms, saw the sneakers and the pulsing eyes of flame in the rope, and understood there was not one thing to be understood ever about the fires people will build who have none in their hearts or heads.

Junior and Minister remembered Lincoln crowing about his sneakers to them all at the consignment-bar, these burning sneakers he said pissed his mother off. ("But what don't?" he had asked.)

Minister remembered taking Lincoln and Woolman and Junior and Lisbet to the playground of one cat-pissed large sandpit and eight swing sets in the commons space of the trailer-park community called Dowless Place. Rocking in the baskets on short chains, flying in the rubber strip on long chains, sky brimming their eyes. He felt how terribly right it was to take the name of Jesus in vain now, now in the country's nihilist hour, at the hour of its death, now at the hour of His death.

"Christ," he said to Christ, "get thee behind me—or—or go fuck yourholyself." His last words sampled something Acker liked to say about the smallest request she resented. He tried on her words and felt ashamed how well they fit.

He took the vapetube from Acker's mouth, had a hit. Hacking painfully as he exhaled, he said, "Good heavens!" He spit up a little Prom, and wiped his mouth with his sleeve.

Mrs. Panther mocked him: *christ*fuck-*christ*fuck-CHRIST.

Other townspeople had awakened. Bunny and the Mister Rounceval came, accompanied by both their deceased parents and another Helltel resident, George Maledon, whom everyone called Arkansas George.

Old OD said, "Not much of a fire."

You're really here? asked Union.

I'm not here, she didn't answer, and not there either.

Just before 4:30 a.m. the unresisting structure's spreader braces and support pieces collapsed, and the long legs and the crossbeam and the flames splashed down.

By 5 a.m. the pool of smoke hovered a last minute before the earth sipped at the low spot where the smoke settled.

Acker said, "UBH," which was like so many things she said that were enigmatic. Woolman seemed to know what it meant, but he wouldn't disclose. One of us could have asked, UBH? UBH means—what?

"Who do you figure did this?" Mr. Panther asked. A curious question coming from a man never seen without his machetes, ideal instruments for hacking down enough wood to quickly fit together a terrible sight like this one.

10.

"Mom? Mom's here—I'll show you," Woolman said, fumbling open his laptop computer. He wore a denim jacket, dark brown with a gloss-white CCR emblem sewn onto both sides of the chest, which had been Stanley Junior's jacket when he was a teen, and it had lived multiple consignment lives. Indulging Woolman's obsession with Oppy, the Opportunity Rover, Acker had sewn on the back the Mars Exploration Rover patch, *JPL MER-B 5352 sols*, which commemorated Opportunity's mission of 5,498 Earth days.

Jacob had asked Woolman about the young man's mother, Marie. The father and son sat within sight of Assorted Wares on rust-crusted Steak 'n Shake stools that no one would buy. Union Vedder, who knew their consignment value, had never accounted for how he came to have them and barter them. You never could figure the like of Union Vedder and, after his deaths, you never could be done with him.

Woolman's mother was a Skype presence in her son's phone and laptop. On rare occasions she came into town long enough to drive Woolman to see something she wanted him to see. She was Administrative Division District Chief for The Pope, and she made that old pigfaced pirate proud. "The Pope" was the nickname for North Carolina's most famous monster oligarch, the most famous and the most hated in the state's history, and it might offer some perspective to remember that infamous list includes Blackbeard. We hate to like such a person. We like to hate such a person. In this part of the South, The Pope is like the Confederate flag that you defiantly pledge allegiance to and defend at moments when your head and your heart are completely and happily empty. In order to guard his wealth, his safety, his fragile sense of superiority, The Pope has his shadows travel ahead of him into the world where he need only meet shadow Popes. Read about him sometime, a man wealthy enough that he owns the rights to your worst cruel impulses, and the rights to making your cruelties and his cruelties seem acceptable and, in fact, preferable. Read about The Pope, and try to continue telling yourself you don't understand how it's possible for people in the modern South to still think being a slave was a free choice made by African immigrants; how it's possible for people to talk vicious trash about the very educators who allowed them to glimpse dawns of self-understanding never before appearing on their horizon; how it's possible people would elect as president a real estate mogul proud of five decades of cheating hired common workers—honest women and men like the Piedmont's workers—out of their hard-won earnings.

On the rare occasions she would see him, Woolman's mother would drive him out to a nearby county to show him a fresh roadside ad for Word of Faith, thriving despite *Constitution-Times* front-page reporting on continuing and new charges of abuse committed by the church leaders who were, it happens, Cord County lawyers with their noses in the Pope and Koch troughs. He would try to ask her the tip-of-the-iceberg questions a teenage boy asks his mother; she ignored him as she showed him the newest private prisons, the newest Quonset hut school additions, and the closed community service centers with closed ballparks and closed swimming pools and basketball courts. Showing him the closed Planned Parenthood centers, she would say nothing about these places where young women might have learned that their choices about their bodies and babies were their own.

She would show him the highway sign inviting young people to join Seconders, the NRA organization introducing them to gun culture. The Pope funded the clubs, provided space for them. Because they offended The Left, The Pope favored most the controversial causes that were often in disagreement with his own personal beliefs. Put small children in promotions for target ranges, in ads denigrating striking teachers; make a shit-in-your-liberal-face roadside poster of grade school children in full MAGA paraphernalia standing in front of a new megachurch. He liked any private invasion signage that cankered the public commons. He gave Woolman's mother a generous commission for setting up all-season signage everywhere in the region. He gave her control over the design aspects of presenting his message, which was this: liberals feel ashamed that they cannot cure or correct or marginalize self-injuring, ignorant, bigoted, working-class nonliberals; the way to politically motivate nonliberals who want to turn their own shame into hate and self-hate is to intensify what Marie called their Cracker Act, which helped them accept further enslavement to men like The Pope all the while they mocked the worst outcomes of wearing such chains.

She wanted Woolman to see what The Pope's long efforts had wrought. She would drive him to the newest The People's Dollar stores in small, impoverished communities far from the chain super-markets. She was proud to oversee the hiring of poor white and Black people in need of work who were deeply grateful to have poor wages, no rights, no benefits, no insulation from reprisal if they blew the whistle. They knew Marie as Miss M, and they showed her obligatory respect.

She wanted Woolman to see: with the help of The Pope she had broken the glass ceiling, she had, in fact, become a person to whom status and money and power had trickled down. Why, she wanted to know, do poor people not seek out tricklers like the Kochs or the Mercers or the Popes or Uileens, like the wealthy lawyer-apostles of Word of Faith, to show them how to be trickled upon? It was, she said, "Beyond comprehension."

While Woolman and Jacob talked, the young man sometimes took a wobbling spin on the stool, which was not properly bolted into the floor and wasn't exactly safe. Woolman's and Jacob's uneasiness about reuniting with Marie was noticeable.

Had his father, Woolman wondered, even liked his mother?

We all knew that the young Marie and Jacob had once, in fact, truly loved each other, and in those days we all admired her forbearance with Jacob, every person's go-to cheap and infrequently reliable household repairman, a storyteller and a gossiper who fit you into his schedule of mythologizing and opining while he sauntered in and around Cord.

We did not talk aloud about Marie and Jacob and Woolman. In Cord some of the older generation still holds back what we could say. We say, "I have a tick on me," which is our expression for having a terrible secret that is, very quickly, everyone's terrible secret in our town of twenty-one hundred. You do not share a tick at first. You wear a tick until it has its way with you or until someone else notices, and then and only then you tell.

Marie had been an intelligent young person who could have gone to college but did not need to, could have kept learning but did not choose to: her version of her story. Before she was married to Jacob, Marie was well liked because her hands and mind solved the problems before her and, as she put it, "didn't wander off into the ether."

She was born again when she reached puberty. At sixteen she married Jesus in a riverside ceremony attended by other restless Jesus-brides and promised-to-Jesus girls and separated-from-Jesus and remarried-to-Jesus women there to watch over her and to be her watching-over chaperones.

Without divorcing the son of God, Marie married Jacob, who was by far "a better fuck," and who did not love her contingent upon her "nonstop knee-killing praise" for him, and who was "anyway, no one's prize."

In those days, more than twenty years ago, she said that kind of thing. We were horrified by her, happy for and horrified by her, though we suspected, we definitely suspected but didn't yet know that Jacob, our town's most prominent loafer, would be our worst jackass.

In 2004 when Jacob left Marie and her toddler a note and nothing else, she did not believe it was a matter for public discussion. She was hard and clean and kept her own counsel, and watched after her manners and tended to her appearance, and helped others but helped herself first. She was only ever quick to temper with Jesus-brides and Jesus-divorcees and with other unJesused childbearing females who were, like her, under complete control while feeling in complete control. If you rubbed her the wrong way you were suddenly, permanently not worth her trouble. She was what a woman handcuffed to Cord must be, a face-eating, throat-tearing creature of God-the-ex who pays Him tribute.

Jacob had now—he had always had—the look of a thirsting man with a glass in his hand and nothing to pour in it.

Jacob had been our son.

Woolman was our son, too.

All that time Jacob was away, Woolman moved into and out of our lives. He was more fixed to our different orbits of influence than the other young people in Cord, who were fastened only to their own families. We made way for him, at first, and, over time, we made a way for him, and he for us.

Until he was twelve, Woolman lived with his mother's only sister, Cee Cee, who had a job Marie had gotten her at The People's Dollar; from twelve to sixteen, he lived in the basement of the Seconders Club in an apartment Marie furnished with chair and guns and table and guns and bed and guns and television and gun clips and other ammunition stored in foam-lined cases and firm plastic boxes. He had his own new guns and full supply of bullets.

He understood firepower.

Marie was pleased that he understood firepower because she felt that at the end, when you couldn't take it all back from the colored people, from the Jews, the Muslims, Mexicans, Hondurans, Guatemalans, Nicaraguans, the shithole countries, you would only have a place to live if you killed for the space, only have people watching your back if they would kill to stand there, only eat if you would hunt down and shoot the ones who were not your kind and if you would eat their kind.

11.

Woolman had moved in with Acker while Lincoln was still living with her. We didn't perceive any jealousy Lincoln or Woolman felt. They had a mutual hobby-obsession with internet NASA reports on the Opportunity Mars Rover, the regions Oppy explored, the sand dunes and dust storms Oppy battled, the newest operational difficulties with the rover arm's instrumentation, with Pancam and Hazcam and Navcam. Oppy, whose life on Mars had started in 2004, was like a slightly younger sister to Woolman and Lincoln who responded, starting when they were six years old, to her posts about her journeys and hardships: injured front wheel, solar panels difficult to clear, repair station malfunctioning. Weekly OUs (Oppy Updates) were quite personal: "Amnesia events today—not feeling optimal. Are you?" and "Soft soil sucks" and "Mud! Impossible! Martian mud!" and "Seventh Martian winter—cold but not lonely. Thank you, Friends!" Each of Oppy's earthtime fourteen birthdays included "Birthday selfie with Billie," and a Billie Holiday classic, "You Go To My Head," sounding in the audiopost as alien to them as secondary X-band radio transmission.

Woolman and Lincoln printed out her selfies with Martian clouds and rock formations, and they posted them all over Acker's Helltel room. When Oppy went dark for a few hours or hibernated for several earthdays, Woolman and Lincoln could hardly bear the return-to-sender crisis; when she came online again, their celebration of the news was that much more intense because it was that much more a secret from their peers who were not Oppywise. Lincoln and Woolman were seven when Oppy's twin, Spirit, exploring the Red Planet's other side, ceased transmission. The boys could count only on each other to understand the private sorrowing that struck when they received Oppy's simple announcement: "Seven kilometers traveled before stopping. Remembering you, Spirit."

After Lincoln was killed, Woolman and Acker kept on keeping house together in that Oppy-shrine environment. Marie and Cee Cee insisted Woolman move out, but that hardened his resolve. They personally insisted Acker quit him, and Acker petted Mike as she explained that she was a person who needed the "sick love" that you know really is sick and really does make you sicker and sicker with love; and she explained that she needed "famous love" the kind you can only have if you're famous and that will make you more infamous all over town.

We wondered about those two and Acker. We worried about Acker's and Woolman's gun stockpile. We knew only a little about Oppy, though we knew she mattered greatly. We talked about what we wondered about, and we settled on the story that for Acker and Woolman to defy Marie, Acker must have a real good understanding of broken communication in deep space and of signal degeneration and of survivability. And of firepower.

And there was the one other thing.

We thought—we were not sure at all, but a lot of us thought—that Marie might have hired some Seconder Club KKK initiates, some teenagers from Mustardseed or East Howellsville or Decker, to lynch Lincoln as a sign to us all that a nigger boy who flaunts the target he wears will be targeted.

Generations of Cord teenagers have been trained in harassing Baracks, which is what the Trumpspawn here calls Black men who don't know their place. You could imply that kind of Black man doesn't know what reparations he owes white people; you could defame that man's family origins and his religion; you could make ape and monkey and macaque jokes and mock-rap rape jokes, and every Cord teenager of every color would hear you loud and clear and proud. They have been trained in intimidating Michelles, which is what they once simply called bitches and now call women of any and every race and background that they treat with respect and even attentive protectiveness *before* the girls graduate from middle school. These particular teenage men have been trained in circumscribing the lives of teenage girls, in bullying nonconforming males, in bearing false witness, in burning buildings; have been taught when and how to sew white robes, how to rip seams and resew, how to stalk and game and troll and gaslight. Their MAGA and NRA and Redditor and Storm Front gear is their gangwear. They are accomplished Seconders.

Cord does not have a Be Best campaign run by a Boy Scout Troop. Cord does not need the usual insignia and uniform and structured activity of a Boy Scout Troop. The teenagers here are good with rope. They are good with militia skills. They know the age-old pledges and tests and the Christian privileges of making the team, of waving their own flags and pennants. They look sharp in church vestments and in the badges and clothes and holsters of law enforcement captains and ranking military officers, in the business-man's shirt and tie and shoes newly shined, in all the uniforms of governing, and in the robes of justice. A favorite name for boys here has always been Jesse or Andrew or Robert or Lee. A new favorite is Donald. And Jared and Steve and Reince and Bannon and Rex and Stone and Roger and Lindsay and Flynn and Kellyanne and Lev and Igor. And Vladimir.

12.

In the evening, the last of the swing set fire had been cleared from the street. Junior and Minister had concluded a meeting of the Festival Board: many of them Regs, some of them musicians or booth-holders; the young ICE-rep real estate agent Covington "Covie" Corsey attended. As room-darkening as bad paneling, Pamela Hayes the single in-residence cleaning crew person for the Helltel, served as the Festival Board Secretary. The day she moved into her second floor room, she had inexplicably posted a large sign: Green Room. If you asked, she said, "I'm no one's assistant, you understand, but I can keep things moving." At the board meetings she expected real business to be in the form of clearly stated board meeting motions and not "blather."

As she left the meeting, Pamela nodded hello to Orelia and went out. Orelia had come to the consignment-bar for conversation with Minister, but they were having none of it until Acker joined them.

Acker brought the diminutive couple bathrobes to try on, since they liked the idea of matching. "We have plague-loads," she said. "I can bring 'em until the sun goes down or this Dark Spell finally breaks." She meant the spell of disharmony cast upon Orelia and Minister by evil red underclothes or a nightlike day of weird weather, but their hearing was complementarily limited and they did not employ the two good ears that together they could lend to Acker.

Acker brought them robes twice and thrice as big as they were. She walked them before Mr. Panther and Mrs. Panther, who croaked approval of Orelia and Minister looking like two old godheads in their monumental forms. She presented the two to The Pines and to the muumuus on the circular rack and to the throngs in the bins. Approval all around.

"You look absolutely mountainous," said Acker, *vhew*ing Prom brew. She had added new piercings to herself, seventeen rings punched evenly around her upper neck, and from each ring a dangling piece of six-inch red string-yarn in a fountain-of-bleeding effect.

"I like you in this look," she said, rearranging Orelia and Minister in a way that made them peak. "You're like my little parents in hell, only littler. They loved me—never read a word of any of my books, never accepted the mushrooms I offered so they could read at least a bittle of The Acker Ouevre, learn some laughing-and-grief, and live to tell. With every new book of mine they didn't read, they grew smaller, I noticed." Acker smoothed one of her yarnstrings with the fingers of both hands, pulling at her neckskin. "And did they notice growing smittler, do you think?

"Did you ever own robes? I forgot what neighborhood of hope they lived in—robes will always help you, but not the shabby ones, they don't help anybody—I remember that trees lined the street where my smittle parents grew smittler and harder and harder and hittler to see, and no one pruned those trees. So the tale goes, the lovely occultations spread their roots and branches and gained great height, and death mated there with death, and nests rocked in almost every branch, and both deaths flew back and forth to feed their deathlings. Wherewhyhow do you think so many people consign their robes while they're still alive? How black Berlin."

When we heard her say things like "How black Berlin," we only understood if she explained. We heard her acroname someone or something "UBH" many times before she explained that as an artist she desired above all else Unnecessarily Brutal Horror. If she asked, "No MAH?" were we supposed to know—without Lincoln's or Woolman's explanation—that she couldn't understand a person's failure to be Mad As Hell?

The enrobed nonce-upon-nonces were paying attention to their dresser, but as for conversation—well, they were not having that. She sold them beers again, which they accepted, the fourth one for Orelia, the third one for Minister.

"There were linden trees, the trees on their street, and that's a kind of tree that makes itself memorable in all the worst ways of being beautiful. Two hours since we started—are you buying? If you're not, finish and get out—oh, oh," *vhew! vhew!* "oh!—I don't mean that—you—you *should* buy these two, they're a steal, they heap you up, you know, you never had this kind of stature before, did you?"

Vhew! Acker's ruddy beardyarn swung like a swished-through basketball net. She held her arms out and did not put them down, one of her most disquieting habits, and she said, "You two want to make a style statement, I tell you you're wearing it—I'll give you a discount for the Pinehurst Paradise emblems sewn on—add up the beer cost—you're outta here for forty total, forty-eight with tip, if not, 'Eat French dip and die,' as my parents used to say in The Large Days."

The small sofa into which they settled was mist blue. She felt that in time they would see why they must have that setting for the sake of their silent majesty. She felt that in her own lives, in the entirety of her life, she had not fallen so in love with two ancient ones. And this reminded her she wished for them to meet *Papilio Polyxenes Keithflynn papilionidae*, brought in by the sofa seller, Horace Cranehelm.

She put her arms down, exhausted.

She drew the swallowtail from its place in the tradition, said to him, "Oh," *vhew*, "oh, you sure are a soar for sighted eyes!" She passed the specimen around.

She read the whole poem, "Baby Boomers," rereading her favorite three lines:

> How is it that a single star
> can suddenly break its vow
> and slide across the entire sky?

Orelia reached into the dark sleeve of Minister. Up she searched until she found him. They held hands. They did not shift position in order to face each other. They did not disrobe.

When they left, four beers later, they were still wearing their robes. Acker helped them clear the doorsill of evening in Cord. Overwhelmed by her feelings of tenderness toward the couple, she looked into the darkness they darkened, and said, "If you were in a book of mine, I'd kill you off right now, right on this page, whatever page we're on, since you are perfect apotheoses."

Intending now to exclude the emblem discount and to include the cost of sofa and sofa-shipping, Acker said, "We'll bill you."

Recognizably happy, incomprehensibly unhappy, they nodded. At a pace three hundred million years slow, they resumed their rocky place on the Piedmont Terrane.

PART II

PART II

13.

In Acker's room at the Helltel, Woolman explained the Skype arrangement to Jacob who had never imagined that in a period of only twelve years virtual teleportation had advanced so far. In 2004 when Jacob disappeared, the teleportation and the thousand other new forms of internet out-of-body experience, including the Book of Face, had not yet penetrated every head and heart in Cord and, so, the recent and the distant past had recessed with less annihilating instantaneousness.

Woolman set the meeting up for 11:30 p.m. Sunday, which was the only time his mother would agree to what she called VAT. When Woolman turned twelve, the VAT, the Value-Added Time, which had been weekly, trailed off. During the past year, he and his mother had seen each other in person for two afternoons. They had briefly Skyped three times.

Jacob did not exactly understand Value-Added Time, and he was not helped at all by Woolman sarcastically saying he was pretty sure the cause was Sharialaw. Woolman performed his best imitation of his mother's free enterprise fundagospelism for Jacob: "*It's shit or it's fertilizer—it's a piece of junk furniture or it's a refurbished hip flip—all a matter of perspective.*" "*If Jesus ain't a brand, Jesus ain't The Man.*" "*Get on your knees and M-A-G-A.*" "*There, you raghead-lover, you gendertrangressor, that's what I mean: Sharialaw, Sharialaw, Sharialaw!*"

"Sharialaw?" asked Jacob.

"Never mind."

The front for her work was The People's Dollar, but her salary was from the Americans for Prosperity Foundation (APF), which gave her flexibility in her assignment as Personnel Coordinator. She spent most of her efforts identifying politically "aligned but unengaged" people among the populations of rural poor and middle-class-poor who could be set afire with hate and who, guided rightly, would spread it like coal ash. Events taking place in churches and community centers introduced Freedom Coaches who gave away budgeting and finance advice (and free turkeys) (and free spiral hams) and hatred (and free tubs of The People's Dollar ice cream) for the government that folks readily believed had made them poor with giveaways to "the lazy people," a description always synonymous with "the Obamacare people," synonymous with "those people" of a different shade than wraithwhite and wrathwhite.

Marie and her peers in APF gave people nutrition and health and lifestyle advice (and free expired grocery items stamped Not Expired) that dismissed the most recent seven decades of science. Free of charge, they gave people self-hatred for how they had been raised God-fearing but had been educated in the public schools to be Godless. They were taught how to use clip coupons (especially for The People's Dollar) as an alternative to food stamps, and were taught that "the takers" who used food stamps or accepted union assistance hated them for their integrity and self-respect and should, in turn, be hated back.

At the weekly free workshops the APF coaches taught them to hate the educators who, so the coaches repeated, taught at the "government schools" that had denied them the rights promised them in the U.S. Constitution (in the APF-redacted version of the US Constitution), which was the roadmap to an individual's Christ-given rights; those who did not want to make America white again, who believed in democracy's commitment to the common good, were hated as mortal enemies of Jesus Christ Masterrace and his disciples.

"Will she talk to me?" asked Jacob, who pictured that her fixed image might appear but not her words. He also pictured that she might have erased him entirely from her thoughts. "Will she see me on this thing?" he asked. "Will she hear me?" And he asked, "Where will she be?" because it mattered where.

"Her territory is big," said Woolman naming North Carolina, Georgia, South Carolina, east Tennessee, southeast Kentucky.

The Skype-ready cowbell sound came. "See yourself up in the corner of the screen? That's what she sees," said Woolman. "Stop moving so much."

"I'm not moving."

"You're wavering."

"Am I?" Jacob saw himself silvery, shivering. His son had his father's narrow face and high forehead, his mother's robust features of strong jaw and Roman nose and straight but not strict posture. Woolman's sea-glass cyan eyes and unsmiling mouth were Marie's; his hair and brows were the red color that certain hawks wear on their shoulders and were uncharacteristic of either Jacob or Marie.

"That's us," said Woolman as she looked directly at them.

The momentary fisheye effect of the computer screen made the evidence of her unsettled mind and heart seem that much more palpable to Jacob, who felt tears come. Her fixed gaze turned him inward to the unlit chambers where they had shifted away from each other, to the half-lit chambers where they could move together in lostness, and deeper inward to the brighter chambers where the two of them had imagined returning to each other.

Jacob blurted, "You are the same Marie, I can see."

Woolman, who had not at all paved the way, said, "We're a family again," and thrust his shoulders forward and barked in a laughing-on-the-leash behavior. "That was fast!"

"I've missed Woolman," Jacob said. "I've missed you, too." He wished he might say something solid, sensible. He looked at his postage-stamp self in the corner of the screen, and he wished he had used some spit on his hair there where it wouldn't stand down. He wanted to look good for M and for Woolman and for the tiny, tiny self whose profile became a blur of grainy expiring match head if he moved too much. He regretted that now, beyond his control, he wavered in the ways he had always wavered.

"We're not anything like a family," she said to Woolman.

"You're a stranger and your father or whatever you want to call him is a stranger." When she leaned in closer, her ears disappeared. The margins of her temples and the line of her jaw and chin became more definite.

There inside the computer screen the freeing-failing quiet felt like the storybook quietings when the cover opens, when a page is turned, when the question ("Life, what is it but a dream?") is asked at the falling-asleep moment, and the covers close.

Jacob said, "Marie, you're—you may be—right."

"Mightcould be," said Woolman, his voice reaching for a specific jeering cruelty he had not mastered to any degree at all.

"We can try. We can try to see what happens next." Jacob asked her and Woolman, "Can we? We're trying, aren't we—we're already kind of trying if you think about it, huh?"

Woolman was reflected on the skittery laptop mirror surface. Woolman was still a young man. And old. Jacob could see that Woolman was nodding his head no, no, they could not try; or, no, he knew she would not try; or, no, they could try but he could not; or, no, all trying for mercy was over in her and Woolman and over and done with in the whole world.

"He showed up in Stanley's~~Acker's~~Stanley's," said Woolman.

"Kind of unbelievable, and Acker—"

"You still with that woman? You are. You are."

"She's—come on, now, she's—"

"Shut up already—you don't know half of what I know, so shut up," said Marie, her wet-look lipstick suited to the Skype-zombie professional manifestation on the tombscreen, and her aloof smile exactly right for someone smiling for her own sake.

Woolman said, "He's staying with Acker and me until he leaves again."

Jacob, who already had a room in the Helltel, had not known of this plan, doubted Woolman had discussed it with Acker. He worried that he would, in fact, leave Woolman after Bunny and The Mister realized he could not pay for his room, but he wished to learn that it was all right for him to stay in Cord with his son, with the people he had always thought of as his people.

Marie said, "I have other appointments."

"She does," said Woolman, "important shit, too—right, Mom? Our time is up, I guess. Time to shut this VAT down."

"Your father tell you how he left—or why he left?" she asked. "He tell you about the voices he thought he heard in the walls? Jacob—speak up. All this time has passed and you got so little to say to us?" Marie brought her open fist before her face and she clenched it and said, "I could break your neck and pluck and boil you and you wouldn't add up to a meal worth my trouble."

Woolman said, "I should—"

"I heard the sounds everyone heard. There's more of those sounds than ever."

"Lost his self-respect," she said. "Lost his mind."

"I lost some weight," said Jacob, aware that any response to her was an absurd effort. "I put on some muscle. I'm not the same as I—"

"He didn't find God and he still put on muscle," said Woolman. "God didn't find him—how do you explain that—twelve years and they couldn't find each other?"

God was in Marie, no doubt. The God in Marie sought God. She was made in the image of God, and that image worshipped God because why not, because it was a waste of time to try to explain to anyone Godless. And there was this new thing Woolman, so tech-savvy, described called HeadOn in which "humans with consciousness but limited intelligence can socialize with artificial intelligences with limited consciousness. No human-to-human access." Acker and her friend Siri favored HeadOn. And there was The Twitterverse and the Book of Face and MomentUs, Marie's best means for herding her APF believers, and she had even changed makeup in order to warm up her metapresence. And that meant God and Marie were disillusioned, alone at an eternally burning brush arbor on earth as self-consuming as it is in heaven. Woolman could see and Jacob could see that together God and Marie were soulless who could have each possessed a soul. Skype, Jacob felt, made it more possible for him to perceive this condition.

Jacob said, "I'm the same but not the same essence, which isn't the best thing, I know, but, Marie, I would like to have something with you and Woolman. You know, something that's not this weird other world inside this computer."

"It's where she is," said Woolman.

"Right," said Marie, though not to either her son or her husband.

Her window closed.

Jacob could feel that she was behind the scrim of the deeper darkness, lingering there, not leaving her own terminal, leaning in where Jacob and Woolman had come to her.

Woolman understood that his fool father wanted the window left opened so the three of them could talk a while longer.

Woolman's thumb swiped a blank space below the keyboard, a small rectangle of recessed metal with nothing at all written on it. Woolman swiped his thumb again, his hands staying, and he looked at Jacob's face but not in the way a son looks into his father's face. *I am lost where you left me*—that was the look.

The Skype bell, an alive darkness, rang.

14.

At the front door of Stanley's~~Acker's~~Stanley's Acker, who had new red yarnings around her wrists and ankles, held her arms far out in order to give herself good crucifamous pain, to "draw attention to consumer suffering" (her words). She was probably joking. Maybe.

She trembled, she sweated, moved her jaw in teeth-grinding grimaces of sales-day greeting.

They had anticipated a full house for the Sale of All Sales Day, taking place on the contemporaneous birthdays of Junior and Minister and the first day of the Soldier's Joy Festival. Clearance Time! announced the fliers posted all over town.

Time sorts it out, and you can bank on that. Time unavoidably swings the disbelievers and the believers alike toward their unfinished business that waits at a time-suspending place: a shower stall, a hearth, orchestra pit, mineshaft, ATM, footbridge, doorframe, an attic, an unlit staircase, a public bathroom, a trench, a barber chair, animal pen, tree bower, e-device, staked garden. A war memorial, a town square, a train crossing, a swing set, a consignment-bar, an unmoored nation.

The unexpected guest awaits the nihilist who has become the fatalist and the fundamentalist; awaits the fundamentalist who has become the fatalist and then nihilist; awaits a nation of us conned by an oaf so cartoonish that with every attempt to spraytan himself to a golden Midas-sheen he becomes more crayon-orange.

Lincoln had been seventeen when he was lynched in 2016. In the months since that event he had not reappeared—not as far as we could tell.

We were watching, expecting. Cord is the dark house of the wounded and the returning wounded; when your eyes have adjusted to the depths in the dark rooms here, they respond to those who never will leave; when your eyes have further adjusted to the span of the darkness, they respond to those who have newly arrived. Union, our consignment haint, was a watcher like no other. Acker, a new arrival to and an ancient eternality in Cord, was a keen watcher. And Mrs. Panther, who could fly through and high over everything. And the Pine family. Jacob, our revenant, was a watcher, too. And Lincoln's mother.

Lincoln had not lived long enough to become a grown man in his own home, and to see Jadia in pictures from long ago, and to think of her as being once vibrant and young.

It could be that Jacob, who returned to us from the outside after all those years of absence was a Presence, which meant he died at an earlier age. It could be that on his journey out of Cord he died in White Oak Swamp or at New Mill Lake. Could be, when a visit from Lincoln's ghost made him decide to return, he died of fright. People here will speculate, that can't be helped. In any case, Jacob was the person we once knew quite well, but not.

Acker was probable but not altogether possible here in Cord, and we figured her to be nine hundred-some years old or three or two hundred, or remanifested in the 1940s or thereabouts. Or a past-her-prime fifty-plus punk, but, well, not.

Mrs. Panther was possibly thousands of years old at the time of her death as the teenage daughter of Minister and Orelia Stanley. Now, Lisbet Pluchet-Stanley, living as a mockingbird companion to Mr. Panther, was nine years old in bird years. Since most mockingbirds simultaneously live a short lifespan of substance and an unimaginably vast lifespan of spirit, you could estimate that in human years she would, at this time, be two thousand and ninety years old. When she flew, the air currents reminded her of seaboard and inland hurricane winds on the oceans in the years before representations of the terrible beauty of the whirlwind could be mass-produced by artists with paper, with ink, with expendable labor. When she cracked seed-shell or insect armor in her bill, inside she remembered tasting the leaf edges of the first pulpit folio of the King James Version. When Martin Luther felt inspired to write his little song, "Away in a Manger," for his two small sons, he heard the castle echoes that she heard and could still remember.

Mr. Panther had a friend in her and she in him.

And why was she indifferent now to her parents, Minister and Orelia Stanley? And to her brother, Junior? She had loved her family members: we had seen how dear they were to her. And in her life and at her funeral, we had witnessed how dear she was to them. And now she apparently felt connection solely to Mr. Panther.

Mr. Panther might be one hundred and fifty or three hundred years old, or older by far. In a crumbling, corrupt town, not yet a ghost town, with so many permanent and visiting ghosts, the list and the guest list get confusing even for Union Vedder, town horrorist-historian.

And who holds the town's hidden stories when the living have put so much effort into burying its secrets and many of the dead are so set on digging them up? And how does any one story in the town go if there are human and animal and vegetal and mechanical ghosts hereabouts about whom the ghosts themselves tell different stories?

15.

So few came to the Sale of All Sales that the whole town, white and Black, seemed absent. Even consigners and consigner-wannabes stayed away, though all of them would certainly attend the Festival when it opened.

Orelia, who had come for the birthday celebrations, said, "I don't understand," and placed herself between Junior and Minister in order to hold her arms around them.

"You know how this tune goes," said Junior. "They'll be back."

"People are ficklepricks," said Acker. "One moment you've got them in hand and the next—"

"They've turned on us," Minister said. He knew, they all knew, the shift could happen with great speed: Stanley's~~Acker's~~Stanley's had been Lincoln's second home, the place where something unholy had happened with that freak woman and with poor Woolman; the place where Jacob, unwelcomed in the community, had returned; the place that was home now to Mr. Panther, who asked too many questions, who didn't keep his weapons at home—who was never one of us—who didn't belong.

Mrs. Panther had flown into the consignment shop with Mr. Panther. She landed upon and scratched at the scalps of the Pine matriarch and patriarch, and replaced their wigs. She pranced on top of the circular muumuu rack. She settled herself in the Belt/Tie/Broach/Scarf/Scrunchee/Bolo bin.

On the rack and in the bin the late-morning sunlight lustered her wings. She encouraged bold style choices for Mr. Panther.

"All things in moderation." That's what Mr. Panther said in accounting for his boring clothing choices.

"Should I go home?" Orelia asked Junior and Minister. She answered herself: "I'll go."

Minister asked if he could see her later in the evening.

She answered plainly and obliquely, "Yes," thinking, *I don't understand us*, and "Yes," thinking, *Come, my confusion, sleep with me.*

As Junior walked her out, Minister Stanley greeted Mrs. Panther. Affection for her came easy to him. Self-doubt, of which he had a full portion, made Minister a Christian certain of his faith and always uncertain of his religion. He was incapable of recognizing this creature, who was named for her association with a panther-man, who was, in confounding fact, his transubstantiated daughter Lisbet, a playful, ominous spectral resonance right here in front of him almost every day.

Minister and Junior and Acker and Mr. Panther tried on suit pants and vests and jackets. Mrs. Panther gave a baleful, tumbling-tempo, crash-buzz-rebound, open-punch beat if the look was in poor taste. Her solo was part of a long Ginger Baker drum solo she had heard through Mr. Panther's headphones. (Mr. Panther was a man of Cream. Mr. Panther was a man of Blind Faith.) She memorized and vamped, she ventriloquated and extemporized as uncaged mockingbirds will do who can imitate a car door slamming, an elevator sticking, a train shrieking forward at maximum speed, a child asking how.

Acker, inside her vapecloud and unselfconscious about stripping her pants off and on, her crimson silk thong-thing a sight to see, needed the proper belts, which Mrs. Panther helped her locate by shaking them one by one from the bin like she was pulling reptiles from their den.

Mr. Panther said, "Miss Acker needs a belt with a lethal buckle. That's what you need, Miss Acker."

Mrs. Panther pulled one for him. "No," he said, "she needs something that if you swing or whip it in front of you just right, it might take off an ear or nose."

Mrs. Panther pulled up something deadlier and something yet deadlier. Neither was deadly enough for his taste.

She raked her bill across a cast-iron buckle that was in the YU?YU? shape of a rude question. He said, "Now, that's got the Ys that'll rip and the—what're those? —question marks? —that'll rip too—that's what you're wanting."

Junior, stripped to his yellowed white cotton boxers, couldn't find the exact right slacks, the golfing slacks he favored. Acker, vapetube still in her mouth, took off the pair she had tried on—men's cuffed, sharp-creased, carrot-colored, like-new—and held them open for him to step into. She closely faced him and he faced her as each foot and leg went in, her thumbnails tracing his ankles, shins, thighs; and when he stood, she shifted her concentration to his body: she folded in the bit of cloth flap, zipped him up, pressed down the metal zipper pull, firmly patted the crotch seam, back to front, front to back, curtain-swept her fingers around the bare flesh of his waistline, the entire ceremony done like a woman would do in a parson's church-bench dream.

Her head appeared to float in her vapecloud, to float and waver and lift. She called her cloud "debbtide" and her vaping "debbing." Junior Stanley, who appreciated the secondhand experience of being in her debbtide, had been astounded when Acker shared information about her debbing dose, which, as far as he could tell, was so extreme it should be brainfatal.

Mrs. Panther, untangling some of the bolos with her talons, asked Mr. Panther a maybe-question about Junior, her older brother: "It-her-bet-her-BET? Et-her-bit-her-BIT?"

Junior had once nicknamed Lizbet "Better," and now he called that to mind, and he wondered why.

And Mrs. Panther wondered when Junior and Minister would recognize her and in what situation. Never?

Mrs. Panther's question for her husband caused them both some kind of mysterious delight.

Only Mr. Panther understood her. He said-sang something—no more than three notes of percussive ornithomusic.

Mrs. Panther sang-said something—no more than three descending notes.

They sang, said, sang.

Mrs. Panther said-sang his three ascending notes. Her head juggered, raised up, juggered harder.

He laughed, a less-is-more, eight-note largo-croak.

They both croaked.

They chee-croaked, choke-croaked. They croaked in the blue-dark ways that "like" metaphors do not help identify. Their dialogue called to mind a scary poem our really old ones had to memorize in the days when children still memorized.

Are there places in this country nowadays where children still come home from school with something poetically terrifying they must commit to memory in order to advance from one grade to another? If not, why not?

In this poem, drizzling rain pours everywhere, everywhere upon the poem's Dark House. ("Everwhere-everwhere-*ever*where!" is what Cord's favorite mythologically eccentric minotaur-teacher Mrs. Strauppiter would say.)

The creepy poem's creepy poet ("The Poemer" according to Mrs. S) has a vaguely creepy buried past, a time when his life has pretty much stopped beginning. (Mrs. S, the Poem Explainer, explained this, her pale claws dipped in the sturdy chalk tray against which she leaned.)

The Poemer tells about being on a bald street on a blank day, and at the front door he can hear Life far away where it begins again, that is, where Life eternally brings the so-called Living back to life, but he, poor Poemer, already knows that he can't clasp the hand he once clasped. In any case, he doesn't have the same heart or hunger ringing in his chest.

The whole thing moved Mrs. Strauppiter to tears no matter how you wrecked the lines in recitation. You did not have to be the brightest bulb in the lamp to feel how she herself stood knocking at the door of that dark house or how she held but did not turn the doorknob on the other side of that door.

It was a life-is-a-bitch poem, which is mostly what you offered in those days to children in the schools that misshaped and shaped them a great deal more artfully and brutally than in these days. The poems were dark houses with wounded, disoriented Poemers glimping from lying to line, which is to say from room to roem.

In our sunlight-striving brains, we schoolchildren brought the dark houses to our own dark houses everwhere in Cord. The poems' shovels of grave-lime stayed in your mouth after you forgot how to say most of the poem's lines. As for Mrs. Strauppiter, she has never left her classroom on the outskirts of town, out by the Old Mill textile building and the ruins of Old Milltown and at the collapsed, fire-blasted structure of the Light of Free Will Baptist, out where the crumbled, empty streets are broomed clean that should be cluttered with years of accreted discardings. The weird cleanness can only be accounted for by the ongoing work of generations of determined long-departed Cord schoolteachers and ministers and threadmill workers and shop owners and pine-straw and cotton and hog and chicken farmers with poems in them berserk-divine as passing bells.

Mrs. Panther and Mr. Panther cheep-croaked, the tone more private.

You keep Death as company in a place like Cord, but it won't always be possible to understand what Death is singsaying. You can't depend upon an interpreter like Mr. Panther, a kind of Special Assistant to The Dead, who came across as an upright fellow but, well ... the mockingbird companion ... and his two Iron Age poem-friends, his machetes.

Acker's hand still slowly rounded Junior's pants, and she noticed Mr. Panther noticing. She was also paying attention to the drum solo sounds, certain passages like over-under and under-over arcs of shrieking cars burning rubber. "What?" she asked. "What? Spill it, Mr. Panther."

Junior had a boner, a small one, Trumpsize. That miniature plug, too, was asking something.

Big dog to little dog, Minister's boner answered with alertness.

Woolman's uncomfortable grunt and Jacob's echoing grunt sounded like roadkill's last release of gas.

The shadows in the room jumped out of concavity into convexity. The cash register opened but with no *ba-ring!* sound.

Union, not responsible this time, politely closed the cash register drawer. The drawer opened.

The register, quiet as rustmotes, should have made a sound, if only a metallic rattle.

A grouping of old-school and new-school large staplers wildly bit down on nothing. The members of the pack kept biting, but made no sound, though they jumped and thrust themselves in every direction.

The clothes rustled in the racks and the items wriggled in the bins and the pull on the fan pulled itself on and off until the fan blades sent a dancing lint-ribbon down, changing the taste of the air, and the wobbly bar stools spun counterclockwise, making the *ba-ring!* the cash register should have made, and spirits fizzed inside the oldest bar bottles, but only the ones with the brand name, *Drinkme*. You've got to ask yourself who could make this stuff up.

A beer mug fell, plinkless, plopless, into the little bar sink where the red lipstick on the rim bloodied the dishwater.

Mr. Panther croaked, "Buy a belt."

Mrs. Panther croaked back, "It's a cinch."

We understood their croaking perfectly.

Mr. Panther croaked, "Want a tie?"

"Not! Not! Not!" Mrs. Panther was, after all, a bird with a sense of mocking humor.

There was nervous but calming laughter all around, including doglaughter. And from inside the walls. From nests of Presences under the building's foundation.

The bricks atop *The Silence That Is Within Us* clacked. They clicked apart. Tumbled off. The overhead fan's tentacle of lint seemed to have caused the collapse, or the sinking beer mug, or the toothless snapping staplers. The sarcophagal volume fell open at the pages where a butterfly had been pressed decades ago.

Without Junior's or Minister's permission, Acker served beers on the house. She drew out the specimen, holding the wax envelope in the light. She read:

> We should admire Rambler roses
> So resilient their vines green what was bare
> ground in a single season, then scale up
> and overtake trees, strangle whole canopies ...

Our mugs went up. A good one, we felt.

Acker identified the poet, *Colias Philodice Rosemclarney Pieridae*, and asked if poets ever escaped naming themselves in their best poems.

And she shut the book upon her. Dust fluttered, dispersed, a flame in a dance with smoke.

16.

The area police and local press, in perfectly aligned agreement, determined the swing set fire had been the work of pranksters, that it had not constituted a threat. Because one incompetent arm of state law enforcement did not know what the other phantom limb intended, the two agents returned to Cord on March 30th; they had received conflicting instructions about which they apparently felt not the slightest discomfort.

The male agent, Mr. Peter Prosdookian, was only a little older than the female agent taking photographs, Miss Alice Bracco, early twenties, wearing what you might call a get-up. Gray pantsuit with matching one-button jacket and polished black shoes. A school uniform, including crisp white blouse—for what ludicrous school of criminal investigation?

They acted as if we had not met them before, this fish-footwoman and frog-footman, these tweedlejabbers. She asked that we call her Al and suggested we address her friend as Agent Prosdookian.

"What else?" asked the right side of Acker's mouth.

"Else what?" asked the left side of Acker's mouth.

The agents had checked into separate rooms at astronomical twilight, the moment of transition noticed by folks here who have learned from the land itself the natural laws of razing. In the morning the two young ones were dosed up on the strong coffee and the oily eggs and apple-buttered toast at the Helltel's complimentary continental breakfast, two neat nonhuman-humans "on assignment" and feeling self-important. *Our two young people* is how we thought of the juvenile agents, since we, memorable as pigpepper, as mousefury, as flapdragons, had met them once before and remembered them perfectly well. Months earlier, these two had been sent to firmly close the case here in Cord, to conduct a noninvestigation of the findings concerning Lincoln's death. They had efficiently done their work without bagging his hands for special later examination, without asking for his phone or for a forensic inspection of his room; without trying to find what box or chair or cinder block he would have kicked away; without canvassing the trailer park residents nearby; without talking to his coach and his fellow football teammates he'd excitedly practiced with for the game the next week.

In November our two young agents had put up the yellow tape around the eight swing sets and the one on the end, the swing set on which Lincoln had been lynched. The tape might as well have marked this crime scene as an Ignore This Ignore This Ignore This zone. The tape should have marked a Here Hatred Hatred Here Here Hatred zone. They did not ask to return to The Swing Playground or Dowless Place Trailer Park for further reenactment of what a reinvestigation would really look like if done with the mission of knowing the truth.

A few hours after their lunch, they conferred at the evidenceless site of the swing set fire.

"You two're at the wrong treacle well with the wrong telescope," Acker said, taking a long deb of Prom, and asking Siri, "Am I right?"

"Well. Wrong," said Siri.

Acker debbed hard, the very picture of vape fixavexation. With Siri's mechanistic sincerity, Acker said, "I will need more information, Siri."

"What are you looking for?" Siri asked.

Agent Prosdookian glanced expectantly at Alice, at Mr. Panther and Mrs. Panther, at Stanley and Minister, at Woolman who was looking at Acker and at Mike.

Alice stroked Mike without asking him to speak.

Siri, hearing Acker talk to herself, said, "Silence: usually correct."

One half of Acker felt to us like a candle going out, and one half felt half-lit.

When the agents' previous visit here had taken place, the killings at the AME Church in Charleston and at the Pulse nightclub and at the music festival in Las Vegas were still fresh in people's minds. There was obvious concern by everyone on the lowest and highest wrungs of the civic leader ladder that in a region like ours—over one hundred lynchings in the Piedmont in the past seventy years—an uninterrupted long record of other hate crimes—a spontaneous public conflagration like the ones that occurred in the aftermath of some of those events could occur at any moment in the tinderbox of North Carolina, its state bird the Outhouse Thrasher.

Alice took more pictures of nothing, of a site without one ashflake of ember remaining. She said, "It could've caught fire to the buildings. I mean it was kinda close to the buildings I mean."

Agent Dookian said, "So little evidence of a large fire. Were there witnesses?"

"I mean," said Alice, "it wasn't a swing set the size of the—I mean of the—the other swing set I mean."

We ignored his question, her observations.

Woolman wanted permission for what he wished to say, and when Acker nodded approval, he said, "Lots of smoke," which Agent Dookian wrote into his notebook.

Acker said, "Weird smoke, you know, Alice."

"Al. Call me Al."

Acker's vape device *vvwhew*ed, and she said, "*Fatal*," which was something positive she often said about her own disappearing and reappearing smokecloud, like the burning swing set smoke but less intrapsychopocalyptic. She mocked Alice: "I mean this smoke wasn't not—wasn't—not like or even unlike the smoke by the way at the—I mean the other swing set I mean."

The smoke they could not see at this site interested both young agents. They said they did not remember smoke at the other site. They did not say it: at the place where Lincoln was lynched. No doubt, that smoke, the other smoke, was not in Dookian's notes, not in Alice's photos of the other site, of our townspeople, including Lincoln's mother, Jadia.

A swing set on fire intrigued them.

A lynching left them incurious.

Lincoln had hung from the north end of one of eight swing sets in a long row at The Swing Playground. There was no smoke drawing attention to the place where the murder happened. There should have been some kind of smoke. We all, Black and white folks, felt it, which does not mean we unequivocally wished for it: the stinking aftermath of hate crime should have traveled out from this place he was lynched, out to the other Piedmont counties, to the other regions of North Carolina and to the progressive South and through the backward, regressing South to the indifferent, smug, educated, and woke city whites and to the hanging-hungry, proudly uneducated and infantilized and evangelized Trumpkudzu white nationalist fanatics of our rural towns. A fire should have caught and overcome the municipal and statehouse buildings and should have incinerated the pointless structures, each of them, foundation and roof and wall.

An intelligent citizenry feeling intellectually superior to intellectually lazy people—if that citizenry reduces the lazy ignoramuses to an abstraction, shouldn't their negligence be called "despicable"?

The special case of an unintelligent citizenry, traitors to kin and country, proud to keep its own children and other people's children in ignorant oblivion—if you call these traitors "deplorable" you have found the right word, haven't you?

When Mr. Dookian asked Alice if she was going to do "more" with him, asked within our hearing, she demurred. His arm almost went around her waist, the toes of her businesslike shoes almost, almost kissed his. For the moment, they were interested in their own but not in our fire.

He wanted photos of the individuals, he said. Her camera remained in the pack with other cameras, even when he pressed his case for getting pictures of us into the files he and Alice would have to submit to the appropriate state investigative agency.

It fell to Mr. Panther to give them some direction. "Mr. Dookian. You believe in omens? Write that down then. Write down, *Smoke*.'"

"You are?"

"Mr. Panther."

"Full name, actual name?"

"Mister. P-A-N-T-H-E-R."

The unamused Mr. Dookian took a note.

"Write us down, little man—how are you going to write us down exactly? Write down our names shorthand. *Smoke People.* That works, that'll do. You met us before. And don't forget Mrs. Panther here; write it down: *Bird? Kind of bird?*—Oh, and those. They're what you think they are, you can keep staring, won't change them. *Machetes. Two.* Write it down: *Two machetes.* You want to take more photos, little Alice? Can you make them look sharp? The blades're sharp from tip to hilt."

"You should see," said Minister Stanley who had never seen them out of the scabbards, though he knew as all of us knew that Mr. Panther used them to chop away at decimus bushes in Ephesus Swamp.

"*Clever* is what you name a sharp weapon. A *handle* attaches to a small blade; *haft* to a large one; *hilt* to a sword. The bladesmith's art of hastening the blade is one of the highest callings." Searching for a way to demonstrate the machete fine arts, Mr. Panther's gaze fixed on Mr. Dookian's forearm and wrist and five fingers as if they were exciseable enemy weapons.

Alice liked Mr. Dookian's nearness. If she would be more compliant, she could have more of that, she knew. She thanked Mr. Panther for his cooperation. She positioned him at the swing set fire, which now could only be imagined. She photographed him with Mrs. Panther, Mr. Dookian once more asking Mr. Panther for his full address and phone number and email, and Mr. Panther declining to provide them.

"You know, Mr. Dookian," Mr. Panther said, "we remember that you were one of the investigators of the—the other event.

"We remember that. You know the shoes on Lincoln—gray sneakers? The sneakers his mother Jadia said weren't his?"

"Gray sneakers," said Mr. Dookian.

"Gray sneakers. Too small for him."

Mr. Dookian's center of gravity adjusted the way a grown man standing beside his mother must adjust to having been inside his mother's womb, while the mother must adjust to feeling the man beyond her remains within. The name Prosdookian was too complex by far, and so we had already named him Dookian because how one names a piece of shit puts a shirt on it.

"When they disappeared from the scene, what did you think? You think you might've found them if you'd gone into some of our new homes, our old ones, our trailer homes, or storage sheds, some of our cars and cars-for-parts in yards by the swing sets?"

Alice looked into her camera at the digital images she had captured. "I didn't focus correctly I mean the—Mrs. Panther I mean she's blurred."

Acker said, "She's vague, isn't she? Mrs. Panther, I mean."

"Blurry," said Alice. "All of this—I mean—this place I mean—the place is blurry."

"Always is." Memories traveled further inside Minister than he had allowed for many years. Mrs. Panther was flying inside him, persistent in her flight. The smoke from the swing set fire still traveled inside, as well. Minister thumped his chest to have some clearage.

Woolman asked Alice and Mr. Dookian whether they might open the investigation again with Mr. Panther's assistance. Woolman was angry, and his words—he had called our two young people "Pretend Agents"—hadn't come out in the way he meant. He said he wondered if Mr. Panther was pretend, too. "Do you three even know each other?" he asked.

"What?" said Dookian. "Who?"

"The townspeople here have the impression that I was one of the original investigators," Mr. Panther said to Dookian. "Write this: *Mr. Panther—liar?*"

Dookian, a dim bulb, dimmed. He seemed not to recognize his own writing, his own hand. At the time of the first noninvestigation, Acker had asked him why he did not question her for the record, Lincoln's girlfriend for over a year. His nonanswer at that time was mildly offensive: "You are approximately twice his age."

She had said, "I guess you've got yourself a whole knotty spool of spunk once you take that kind of fact into consideration." And why implicate a white woman? was what she thought.

"I might've misled you," Mr. Panther said. "Might've misled them, too."

Mr. Panther smiled in a friendly manner, and how could we help but smile back? It was news to us that Mr. Panther had come to Cord under false pretenses.

You'd think we might take offense at him suckering us in the ways that would make us vulnerable to him. Instead, we smiled, and we glanced at each other for the signal. Was or was not Mr. Panther a Presence? We already felt that he had arrived the way other Presences arrived: from beyond us, from among us, a serious threat to us and a strange comfort.

Alice again posed each of us, took the pictures, full body and head-shots, that would accompany Dookian's notes and her own.

Acker asked Siri, "Do you want me to continue?"

"I have everything I need already," Siri answered.

Posing Acker for a photo, and that not going at all well, Alice asked, "Born here? Not? I didn't mean don't mean anything you know what I mean—do I know about you?"

"Silence: usually correct," said Siri.

Acker's white makeup and blue lipstick. Her kid gloves. Her platinum hair pulled forward and high up, throwing a caul shadow over her face. Her vapecloud hovering around her, not a smoky cloud but a vaporous one like the lightest last fog lace coming apart in forestland. She must have been particularly difficult to shoot. "You don't know. You don't read the great books is my guess, Alice-Alice-Al-Alice-Al. Because. I. Was. By the way. A. Fucking. Phenom. Major. Firebomb of The Literary Cruise Lines. Eh, Mike?" She gave Little Mike a firm patting and an upward-stroking fingertip petting, pleased when Mr. Dookian noticed. "A. Fucking. Monstercunt-Mothership-Dark-Farce-Taser. Did my pirate thing. Ripped out the usual furnishings of the publishing mansions. Rolled the treasure-hoarder bookclubbers for their small loot. Sunk the old fleets of old fuckfarts sailing the tired, tame overcharted mildwaters of the meta-arts. I. Am. Fucking. Major. *Here. Be. Dragon.*"

"I mean—you were—famous?"

"Shit yeah." Acker took her iPhone from Little Mike's maw, and she gazed in, asking her own image, "Do you look not-famous to me?"

Siri answered, "This is about you, not me."

Acker laugh-croaked, and Mrs. Panther croak-laughed and Siri, still on tap, said, with no trace of human affect, "LOL."

Acker returned Siri to Little Mike. From within the pouch, Siri said, "Hee-hee. Hee-hee."

17.

In the evening Mr. Panther and Mrs. Panther and Acker and Woolman walked with Alice and Dookian to the Helltel where the young agents could have a late dinner and rest after their long day. The Festival had opened at 5 p.m., the music on the main stage fountaining in pulses, the first pitches and sales and failed sales could be heard, and someone said, "What is that?" and someone else, "Tastes good," and an unadorned scale of fiddle music chasing another related scale offered splashcleaning dialogue.

Mr. Panther took their hands into his. He held the cool hands, turned them palms up so they could see the moon there, the light of the first waxing crescent. "Take a note, Mr. Dookian—might be an omen of unfinished business."

Huh? What the fuck? is what Alice and Dookian thought. They said nothing.

They found themselves mesmerized by their hands.

They wanted their hands back.

He had not let go of them. "Are the twilight and moon phase the kinds of thing that matter to you like they matter to me?" Mr. Panther's tone was firm. "Do you ever think about the times when the light is just right for us, for you and me, for the lives ahead and behind and under us, and we can come out of hiding?"

Mrs. Panther flew up, a space-shot launch, her body moving along the line of the earth's curve, and relaunching, her wings defining vapor-trail, dark tendrils, her talons making an effort to perch on the moon's brightening tip.

"You ought—" He changed his grip on them, two awkward pieces of luggage.

"By the way, I live here in the Helltel," said Acker. "Good place for visitors. Ant problems, though. We'll check your drapes and drawers for you."

The Helltel's windowlight failed, the façade of seventy eyes flickering awake and back to sleep. If Mr. Panther held their hands less tightly, Alice and Dookian would have reached for their keys, real metal keys attached to the modern plastic card keys that never properly worked. Under the low awning, he had shifted into a shade that more fully pulled them in. They could see neither him nor the door before them.

"You can let our two high-level top-security government officials go now, Mr. P," said Acker.

He dropped their hands. Dead weight. With one shrug of his shoulders he flew up to be with the moon-canoeing Mrs. Panther, or—or at that moment he turned away from them, or for an instant to which their eyes could not adjust, they lost him—or the teeth of the overworld gripped him so well that he disappeared in its mouth.

"Come to my room later," said Acker. "Two zero two. We'll have a room service feed, we'll shower together, dig out our devices to return Mom and Dad's calls, and do some cold beers with the TV news, and check in with Oppy, tonight should be optical depth tau, a good time for Oppy transmission. You know Oppy? What world're you from?"

Dookian's and Alice's hands had been so suddenly released by Mr. Panther that they remained in the air where they held darkness.

"We'll snort some cookie-dough ice cream and some magic-blue icing, my treat. Fluff our shit up for sure. Deb alittle, deb alot. Climb each other like adjustable ladders, i-film the good parts slow-mo, listen for the train to come through town, I mean I probably got the order of events wrong but I mean I'm imaginative if you know what I mean. Oh, and by the way …"

Spells always offer an *and* that adds nothing to nothing, and a *way* that continues from nowhere to nowhere. If you want to prove it to yourself, put yourself nowhere—stare awhile at the empty sky or at the dirt or at the edgelight around the dirt at your still feet. Now, repeat the word *oh* or the word *or*—and, oh, add *and*. Add *and*.

Add *and*.

Add *and*.

You will find yourself flying, you will find yourself far under.

The young agents had planned to investigate Ephesus Swamp in the morning. They had decided against that plan—not time enough, they felt. Alice said, "I didn't bring the right clothes for swamping," and, imitating some television version of a jaded investigator, Dookian said, "Swamping alone is never a good idea, my dear." The decision process made them feel amused: they sounded clever and light in each other's company; they felt they were where they should be.

Their hands hurt, one spell replacing the other. What Alice and Dookian had seen the first and now the second time in Cord had hurt them underneath the insulation of their fake professionalism, and they felt the bruise in their hands. Acker's enveloping vapecloud made their sinuses and lungs also hurt. They imagined—must've only imagined it, right? —that Mr. Panther and young Woolman wished them harm. As they entered Room 202, not resembling either one of their own rooms, the sharp, good, all-day adrenaline taste of their low-burning fear converted to some other dish.

"Oh—oh—oh by the way," said the Ackershadow inside the vapor or the vaporAcker animating the shadow. And led them in. And led them in. Or showed them the way.

18.

Jadia Lennox didn't understand what led her from her home to The Passages, the places of returning and releasing for the consumed whose souls are given no time to burrow in or fly beyond. It was not Lincoln who brought her, not Lincoln who met her there, and she couldn't understand what could keep her son from reappearing in Cord where so many reappeared.

When she had told Minister Stanley and his son and the other people and Presences at Stanley'sAcker'sStanley's that she was going to the secret swamp places, they knew she wouldn't reconsider.

They supplied a three-in-one thermos, a backpack, a frontpack, light tarp, a battery-powered camping lantern, a two-day supply of dried fruit and jerky and a consignment-item water bladder of strong Mugwort tea. A person repossessing is twice-possessed in the supermassiveness of places like Stanley'sAcker'sStanley's.

They asked her to take Webb and Mrs. Panther with her—as what? —witnesses?—assistants? They must have felt that Jadia would discover more of her own courage in the incautious company of fearless nonhuman once-humans.

Acker had several bad ideas about what else—pistol, ax, bear spray, tire iron, other defensive tools—Jadia should bring for the days she would be gone. Jadia had never liked Acker, who always gave her reason to like her less.

The rubber boots Acker fitted Jadia into were Junior's, but she insisted they be contributed to the cause. "And you need some ruby slippers, Jadia."

Acker had taken all of Dot Nolo Doyle's slippers and other Mardi Gras artifacts on consignment when Dot's two-year cancer remission ended. (Dot's marker out at Harmonist Cemetery offered her birth/death dates and "HIP," which either designated her self-perception, or stood for Hell In Peace.)

"Not? No slippers? Okay—not."

Acker knew Dot's and Jadia's shoe and clothing sizes were identical. Before even Dot knew, Acker knew that Dot's cancer had returned: Acker had a dream of Dot's favorite muumuu levitating before The First, The Seventh, and The Final dream-realm judges who unanimously decided her gown (Carolina blue with an artsy red rosebud pattern that looked like blossoming scarlet bullet holes) was in poor taste.

Dot's consignment arrangement with Stanley's Acker's Stanley's was not as strange as it might seem, since the understanding was this: that after death, Dot would return and would receive her consignment profits; that late in Dot's next manifestation as a Presence, Death would then return for Dot but draw out the dying; that each time Dot would consign but not resign; that her cycles of hell-going and hell-leaving would repeat. Remittance is the natural order, we all know that.

Acker also provided the youngest Pine family member for Jadia to take along. She removed his brunette Prince Valiant hairpiece. Since the family members shared the same shoulder, it was necessary to rip the youngest up by the throat.

"You ever *not* high, young-lady-or-whatever-kind-you-are?" Jadia did not hand back to Acker the lifeless, wigless Pine.

Low in her frontpack, the head, about the size of two adult fists pressed together, shifted there. A young thing, the top of the head splintery from dry thoughts.

Young Pine settled.

Young Pine shifted.

Union followed, talking to Webb and Mrs. Panther. They walked on Sweet Thorn, passing rows of festival booths, hearing the music behind them, a fiddler out of tune, a food barker sounding bird-shrill, a singer off-key.

They entered a large outer area of crop pines, perfect tall soldiers. Since she was a child, Jadia had seen this strict formation, many collars of trees. As the ranks thinned and relaxed, you came to the places where only slumping tree wrecks stood in boggy depressions. As saplings, the slash pines had been harvested from the natural forest and replanted in order to grow a regular crop for pine straw and cheap firewood. People here, resourceful beyond imagining, have always held on, even when another restless, rote-learning generation has cried, "Keep up!" and has progressed, and is gone, long gone.

Union stitched his way into Jadia's wordshreds. Some of her rage rode on the news she had seen that morning, and he had seen it, too, and outside of her lines of thought, he crayoned in his own rage about the Trump Reich's high priests: the cannibal leprechaun Speaker with blood gobbets always on his chalk-white cleft chin, and the pale, skeletal pussy-grubbed Spokesbimbo, and the gasping, writhing flounder-eyed Press Secretary, and the shuffling, scab-face, wart-head Fixer who assigned himself the pirate moniker Bright Bart. And, barely visible though ubiquitous, the smiling anti-Christ shadow president, the Rabbi J, accompanied by his wife wearing one of her flirty silhouettes in the Kors-abuses-Herrera style.

Would any of you—would you give my boy one devil's second ever up there, making your plans high up there? You—any of you give him one share of one second in your tower where you talk up your deals and take your cut? You—you? What hate you serving up—what lying bigotshit comes out you—what bullying nazi vomit—what ants crawled off you onto my Lincoln?

God ever mention my boy to you up there high up there in your Trumptower?

And Union's voice joined hers: Up there where you're spying on undressed teenage beauty contestants, pawing under airline passenger's dresses, paying someone's enslaved Russian teenage daughter to dance over your grin and piss on you.

All your Pharoah's army up there with you?

Your sycophant tea-party clubhouse buddies. Your nationalist cable network co-conspirators.

Once she discerned that the leaf dancing through the currents in her flooding head was Union, she accepted him there. After all, Union was a harmless force in the world all his life. He had accepted that being harmless is a particularly awful verdict for a man. Being harmless will get you shunned by young women and by other young men, killed in war or in the streets, preferred by middle-aged harmful male and female bosses, shown no mercy by your adult children for your failures, assigned as the witness but never the wit nor the warrior nor the bedmate in every story you hear or tell of people's power to do damage.

Afternoon light moved in a tapestry pattern over the ground. They were walking through something more like unfurling fabric than forest. Webb barked up at Union, ran ahead, asked about the pissing-on enjoyed by the piss-partier-in-chief of the former U.S. democracy. This golden shower fact concerned Webb, a four-legged pisser who could not imagine choosing to be the pissed-upon, and Webb anxiously asked, When does something like that start, when've you ever seen it, do you remember Dot's muumuu with the Bacchasauruses printed all over it, or the one with the pattern of hairy man-udders on the front and back, or the one with the world's most famous fountains, they come to mind, things like them can't go in the trash, too beautiful, lard-spit and bacon smell in the cloth, lint-glue on the hems, vinegary underarm stains—Jadia could kill someone, ought to stop her before she does—you notice this place has no place to rest safe, ground's cold, air tastes the way frozen mudcake tastes, no good salt for satisfaction—pissed on by a young one is better than an old, I guess, I guess, I wouldn't waste my piss on that orange fireplug—Dot had one muumuu with dog biscuits printed on, pretty unappealing—best to ignore Mrs. Panther who nips me, no lie, nips me between-on-behind the ears when no one's looking, thinks she's flirting, it's sick—that poor Jadia needs to bring down something big and pretty soon in order to have some revenge for her son who's bigger than the biggest thing any human ever buried—does she know you're along? Union?

Union?

Union?

Union answered no. Jadia sensed the path of his words splining the grooves in her words, his listening presence. All her life she had her own paths to walk, and the words of her son Lincoln were the ones to which she was most attuned. She had a simple question she asked him from the time he could first understand: "What direction you going?"

When he first crawled, first walked. "What direction you going?"

When he decidedly did not like learning fractions. When, on the basis of baked Brussels sprouts, he felt God was untrustworthy. When his chores did not get done. When he wanted to eat crap or hang with crap or talk crap. When he wanted to upgrade the family computer so he could travel craters with some robotgolfcart somewhere moons apart from what matters on this earthdirt on this here ground right now. When he thought football practice mattered more than homework. When he didn't like her giving him so many damn directions about self-respect, about curfew, about listening good when his mother or his teachers or the minister talked.

When he befriended Woolman, the boy with the missing dad. When he went under the spell of the thing Acker, went to work at Stanley's ~~Acker's~~Stanley's, made himself a kind of second family there.

She asked him the question, "What direction you going?"

She carried his answers and nonanswers inside her, replayed them in order to know she heard them right.

What direction?

Where I see it's clear ahead.

What direction?

Mom—you know… You know…

Where I got no other choice. Where I'm close enough.

Close enough? For what?

To make it back to Cord, Ma. To see to you.

Ha!

To—you know—ask you for directions about what to do, how to reset?

What in God's name did that mean—reset? What direction should *she* go now that she had walked so far in?

In his direction, no matter how.

19.

Jadia heard the singers, the fiddlers, the barkers, the festival too faint to trust as parts of a real event. She heard the barking of Webb, a kind of dog she had always heard called a mountain feist. She walked along Lamp Creek toward the bog where Lamp and Feed Sack Creek and Anhouse Creek merged, not remembering to eat, remembering the verse from Second Corinthians for which Anhouse Creek was named, not drinking her tea, revisiting a conversation with Lincoln, the last one, in which she asked about his friendship with Acker and Woolman and their friend Oppy, and was that working out, wasn't that a problem, did Acker have a whole name you ever heard? "If Oppy's an 'avatar but real'—what that means is ... help me here, help me. How am I supposed to know what that means?"

She had asked, "Do you all four have to go everywhere together like you're in grade school?"

"It's all cool," he told her. "It don't look it, Ma, I get where you're at. But we're like what you call the wheel inside the wheel."

"You're somebody else than yourself if you're always attached like that," she told him.

"I'm here now, Ma. Just me."

"Want some tea?"

"What kind?"

Picky as ever, aren't you? she thought, and said, "Mugwort."

"Mugwort," he said. "That'll make you crazy."

"I called something 'the wheel inside the wheel'?"

"Mugwort'll make you see things—you told me that. You're always calling something the wheel inside the wheel. You always say that when you look hard everywhere you see the wheel inside the wheel." He gave her the chin-up nod that was his thing. "You're probably right, is what I think."

So few nests in the trees. So little music coming from the air and the ground of the swamp, except for what Mrs. Panther offered and what Webb obliterated with barking back talk.

Well, I guess I'm full of it. I can't have it back, can I, what I said that was so full of it. Made no sense ever—wheels inside wheels—in the heights and the depths guided by angels—governed by God for the best. Too much church too many years.

As if he were Ezekial himself, Union set the gyroscopic sentence in motion in her head where she could not possibly welcome it now: *The appearance of the wheels and their work was like unto the colour of a beryl; and they four had one likeness: and their appearance and their work was as it were a wheel in the middle of a wheel.*

Mrs. Panther began singing in the air and calling from the tree branches. She stayed mostly within Jadia's sight and hearing. Jadia now walked with no direction, though her purpose was the same. She wished to walk until she could be found by The Passage where Eedie and Eddie drowned in 2007. She had never been there. A foul, snake-infested bog, she thought, was God's design. And I'm askin' straight up what does that say about you, God?

For we know from chapter and verse, that if our earthly house of this tabernacle were dissolved, we have a building of God, an house not made with hands, eternal in the heavens.

Union's thought echoed inside hers, a satisfaction for them both, for two people of the congregation who loathed and loved The Book's bluest tongues of flame within its tongues: *For what is your life? It is even vapor that appeareth for a little time, and then vanisheth away.*

Union remembered in the same way that Jadia remembered when some reporter for *The Bridger Weekly* had described the deaths of Eddie and Eedie in a darkly romantic Veterans Day Heroes story from which the reporter had subtracted the story of their drowning in Ephesus Swamp two days after returning to the U.S. from duty. The reporter wrote in the manner so-called reporters will predictably always do in a war-related piece; he included a tightly focused stock photo showing a shiny, unbloodied folded American flag in a disembodied survivor's lap; the soldier is portrayed as unimaginably miraculous in her/his battle to return to the living; a wannabe-movie-star pastor/minister/priest provides the quotable default "greater love than this hath no man" patriotic commentary; in such articles everyone who is in on the horrifying joke does not acknowledge the war mission was, after all, a risible cruelty played on gullible families and promoted by a malleable news media and celebrated by a recruitment-ripe community proud of feeding so many unemployed and unemployable young people to the unspeakably politicized military.

Webb led. He looked behind him often, barked in order to ask if they would rest, why not, hot out here, muggy, paws sticky, can't exactly change my coat, can I, no hurry to get there, no schedule, right, bugs eating my anus, my nose, my eyes, my package, but no hurry, no hurry, right?

Union reminded Webb it was all up to Jadia.

Webb asked Union if he knew why people who gave their dogs everydamnthing never gave them dog mirrors, why not, or extra bowls to bring things to instead of dropping them down between human feet, stupid, undignified, it comes to mind, or why not a cup of strong coffee in the morning, or toast, dry is fine, or newspaper, hymn book, magazine, modern poetry delivered to the doghouse or dogbasket, novel, some iPad, some Kerouac, some classic dharma porn—if the pissee-in-chief never had a dog friend, not once, not one dog companion, what human could trust him—if his lies left stink on him of course it left it, that would be too much stink to miss unless you stank like a donkey's tonsils—don't ask, don't even.

After hours of walking without stopping, Webb became more difficult. His circling around her and his circling scent-searching just beyond her tightened, and he was deliberately underfoot. He whined. He slowed down. He ignored Mrs. Panther, focusing his attention on the creek, on the creek bank.

From the shade of the slash pines, they came into a boggy cauldron of late-afternoon light, blasted roots and limbless tree trunks thrust up like rusted blades in swollen fists.

The sounds and the smells were disagreeable, Webb felt. He raised his nose up into other less noxious webs of air near a cluster of decimus bushes. Mrs. Panther missiled over him, plucked a cork-screwing silver hair from his brow.

Fuck that! Fuuuuck thaaat! Hurts!

Webb pushed his body against the part of the bank toward which he had more or less led Jadia. He stayed.

Union, who knew this place in the swamp, said, Webb, you fool dog. Not here.

Walked dayandaft, it'll be night before you know it, night and dogeaters out that'll eat your soft parts off, can't you smell eaters in the air, something killed over and over, no smeller at all on you I

97

guess, no way to beware what comes next from behind where some-meansomething'll be killed that'll already be dug up, dragged out, nothing fresh-killed here.

Tomorrow would've been better, said Union. She would've been a little more ready.

Bad places like this, you dog them they dog you, you leak on a tree it's leakin on you, little stickly sticky stanky plants here pretty enough to notice, you just saw them, they saw you, what you brushed past poisoned you, what you walked past passed you, people never think you don't want to be walked, you've had enough of people using you for an excuse to get away from people with people fever, never let you rest, never offer an honest dog a tortilla warmer or a chewable used dildo or a boombox or a cold stick of butter in its wax paper diaper, I mean it, who likes places like this, I mean, nobody ever.

Fool dog. Union remembered the noble wolfhounds and greyhounds memorialized everywhere in Arlington cemetery. He remembered the Civil War stories of noble dogs eaten at Vicksburg by the starving Ohio 83rd Regiment.

Webb would not move from the bank. Jadia touched the smooth, cool head of the young, faceless Pine. "Want out?" she asked. She did not want to rest. She asked herself and Union and Webb and Mrs. Panther, "This is it?"

Ten feet in the air, a rope swing was suspended from an oak limb reaching all the way across a deep, rank pool. Strong as a trapeze bar, the swing was perfect—it is perfect yet—on the nights of the first waxing crescent moon—for wild, fatal flight, for calling down the stars.

20.

Jadia drew Young Pine from the backpack. She held his cool head in her hands, turned him. Her three days in Ephesus Swamp made her feel she had tagged a post and run and run from that timeplace and returned and returned and returned without remembering the first tag and turn.

"I need to ask you about my son," Jadia said to the two, Eeedie in bra and panties, Eddie in boxers. Young as in all the newspaper pictures of them, two detonating blossoms. Reposed. No hair, no ears, no feet, no fingers. Their black-icicle legs dangling. Their black cornea and black sclera at a glistening melting point.

21.

When the moon brightened the swamp, Mr. Panther could more easily find depressions that formed dry or watery brightening eyes. His flashlight enlived the shadows of wrecked trees guarding these places, the vinecurtains in the air and upon the ground, the inter-connected systems of webveils. He had covered the flashlight lens with a homemade red filter in order to recognize devils in the details.

He and Mrs. Panther had come to The Passage where Eddie and Eedie kept watch. In the darkness, completely obscured from Mr. Panther's view, Jadia now talked to herself and, so it seemed, to Union Vedder as well.

You lost? asked Union.

"I have business here," Mr. Panther said.

He has business here, said Union.

"Well, I—"

"Lost," said Jadia. "Here nearly every night with his birdwife flying over him, his red beam cuttin everwhichways, and his machetes chopping at the little decimus bushes. Lost."

Union said, Listen, we don't mean to be cruel. You know what you're looking for?

"That's my—"

So you're here night after night. You're a businessman here in the Piedmont, here in Cord —in Ephesus Swamp—deepest part of the swamp. As you can see, this is a corporate-friendly paradise boom-ing with business opportunity. This little small-business hub is the place you've got business?

"Yes."

You're going to come back here night after night, said Union, until you've found what you're looking for.

Mr. Panther said, "I kind of know you, don't I? You're Union Vedder—never seen or met you, but I believe I've felt and kind of known you."

I'm around.

"You are. You're around." With the ludicrous intuition we low-gain human antennae trust, Mr. Panther scrutinized the geology his flashlight's beam could bring into his field of view and, so, his senses: the mild watery eruptions and craterings, the dense surface coverings of needles, bracts, tufts, capsules, catkins, and drupes, the heated odors and aromas of decomposing and regenerating processes ripping raceme sutures and brightening gauzes of pollen, the sounds emerging from collapsing altars of rotting animal and vegetal offerings, the syrupy tears pooling in chambered stem pith and in the cups and overcups of nuts.

You understand, said Union. I haven't gone away—that's the sim-plest explanation of me. I haven't. I don't. Won't.

"Ain't here to receive visitors," said Jadia. "Excuse me."

All trace of her was instantaneously gone.

She suddenly returned in order to lightly touch Mr. Panther's shoul-der. "Tell my people I'm alive," she said. She might have moved her face close to his. He felt he had imagined her breathing close to his ear and neck: the air intimated a voice, a breath; the darkness rested upon and lifted off him.

"They—we want to know what's going on with you, Jadia. That's all you want me to tell folks? That you're alive? When will you come back?"

Jadia would not answer.

Mrs. Panther's distant chalkboard cryskree reminded Mr. Panther that she lived in the imaginal wilderness he could access only through conscious effort. "I need." He turned off his flashlight in order to better see the darker resins in the sediments and precipitations of the many darknesses beyond and nearby. "I need." His own wet gasp and tears made him reach for support and, finding none, he fell into the muck and, as quickly, rose up on his knees, stood up wobbling, trembling. "I could be—can't quit—I could be close to finding them," he said. "Started looking for them before I ever came to Cord."

Tell me, said Union. It's not like I don't know, but if you don't tell me, I have no certainty I can help you.

Mr. Panther pointed his flashlight at two spindly decimus bushes, and moved closer, causing their cast shadows to elongate in the beam of light. Wind, it seemed, had made the bushes gatherers of rag fibers and feathers and shreds of grocery bag plastic. A thick vine had climbed into each bush, but the particular kind of fibrous growth did not seem the same kind as the other vines he had seen on all of his nights of searching.

The decimus don't belong, said Union. Invasive, he said, they're everywhere you look, and their flowers stink. They say the hips on them make a good tea for toothache problems. They say the roots are nothing like the branches. They—

"And that vine? I've never seen a vine like that one. I almost cut it."

Mrs. Panther now flew so far above him she was a jittery penciltip moving in a note-taking pattern on the sky's paper. Mr. Panther gave her a command that sent her higher. "I love her," he said, "but she's impatient."

And when did you start looking? asked Union.

"Can't see you," said Mr. Panther.

Me either, said Union. I'm almost-but-never, I'm ready-formed-al-ready-faint. When? When did you start trying to find these bushes, the first of these decimus?

Mr. Panther lifted his right machete to cool his face with the blade, or to wipe tears away. The tip of the blade lifted his left eyebrow. He bowed his head slightly in order to bleed good and be relieved. Blood flowed into his eye, ringed his lower eyelid. "June 15, 2015," he said.

These are the two?

"They are," said Jadia. "I don't know how I know, but I know."

"Hello, Jadia," Mr. Panther said.

"Hello."

You figure out when they came here? Union asked.

"Soldier's Joy Festival, same year."

You come back here as soon as you can. They're not going anywhere. Union asked, Am I right?

In two languages of shadow, Eedie and Eddie answered Union, "Fuck.You." They had not wanted to give up the bodies of the two young women, Joan and Karen Little, Mr. Panther's nieces who had disappeared from his brother's home in Washington, North Carolina. Only Eedie and Eddie and the killers had known they were brought here, the lynching ropes still around their necks, planted here with decimus bushes marking their places of burial, with the rope-end vined through the bush limbs in case the bodies should ever need to be pulled up and hidden somewhere else.

Union said, You've got them marked now. You can come back for them.

Jadia said, "Go, Mr. Panther. Tell my people about me, okay? Give them this." She handed him Young Pine, the proof of Mr. Panther's contact with her.

She was near. He searched with his beam of light, couldn't find her. Of course not, he thought, she's all gone.

22.

On Tribute Day, the fifth day of the festival, war veterans were asked to gather on the stage for the sunrise blessing given by Minister Stanley. When he observed how cranky the vets were that the event planners had made them get up so early, he said, "This is the day the Lord has made. We have our loved lost ones with us on this day. At our sides, we have Eddie and Eedie and all who have been buried here still alive as ever." He had meant to say "carried in our hearts" and because he couldn't undo the error, he asked for the anthem.

The national anthem always causes our sleeping to deepen. Like the sleepers in all fairy tales, we have been under a long spell, and our anthems to democracy are only as familiar to us as the Directions for Use printed on our medicine bottles.

Dookian and Alice had dreams in which their necks were stretched by strong leather belts attached to the ceiling fan noose-dancing their smoldering bound bodies around and around room 202. On each ankle they wore fifty-pound dumbbell weights.

They were completely naked except for gray sneakers, not theirs, two sizes too small. In the back palates of their mouths they gargled sharp chips, their own teeth. Their swollen lips were stiffening, and the displaced bones in their faces rupturing, collapsing. On their closed eyelids and eyebrows and inside their seeping ears and nostrils they wore ant swarms, bite-sipping blood that had come to the surface.

They could hear hard, insistent knocking in their chests while their bodies remembered once standing alive atop the world's trap door.

Their spines loudly sang, Hee-hee. Hee-hee.

Their lolling tongues tasted coffin air.

Grubs cleaned their gums and inner cheeks. The tips of their noses and the lobes of their ears were liquifying. Worms turned in their frenula and eyesockets, inside their middle ear canals and other viscid orifices.

They heard, *Mistaker? Mistaker?* and were sure the sound was made by eager, clicking, armored throngs hatching inside their soft humanness.

No surprise. No surprise in any of this.

They had the very same dream of being assaulted with planks, hammers, pliers—and what are the odds of that, unless you account for the oddness of them in actuality awakening in Acker's hotel bed where the two were intimately pressed flesh to flesh, Dookian over easy atop Alice.

From not more than nine feet away, Bunny Rounceval and The Mister Rounceval repeatedly knocked and called at the door, their clicking dentures adding emphasis: "Miss T-acker? Miss T-acker?"

George Maledon, the presence in room 204 (solely his room for over six decades) had called down to the reception desk to complain about 202: laughter, terrible shrill laughter all night long. "Awfullest thang," said George. When he was alive, he had told us that growing up in Hawksbill, Arkansas, he had "seen me some Real Awful."

Acker was not in the room. The Rouncevals found, instead, the two knocked-out young agents in an x-marks-the-spot configuration of inverted naked embrace on the bed. Alice lay face up underneath the hirsute, prostrate Dookian. Secured with clear packing tape, her hands gripped his sneakered feet, his hands gripped her sneakered feet. They were taped at their spread-eagled legs and arms. They were taped belly to belly.

Their phone devices, taped and overtaped onto their lower backs, tee-heed loudly. The female tee-heeing of Siri.

Dookian and Alice faced, as never quite before, life's points of egress and entry.

"Look here!" Bunny pointed at the treasure before her.

"Beautiful," said The Mister, whose appreciation for the young increased in tenderness as he and Bunny pushed toward eighty-five. You could not discount the beauty of the bound young couple, their linkage very definitely a poem, that is, a communion of like and unlike that cannot and must not and must and will join, and at the places of joining will and must and must not and must fall away instantaneously, the heart of the person inside the poem plummeting.

They loved poetry, Bunny and The Mister—everyone could always tell it. Their teacher, Mrs. Straupitter, recognized that they were sweet on each other even as children. She felt great distaste for their innocent love of poetry and their puppy love for each other, which took the form of them hungering for each other's company while treating each other horribly. She called their parents to the school, referred to the infatuated children as Bug and Bug Spray, made warnings ignored entirely by the parents, who had been Mrs. Straupitter's unhappy pupils decades earlier.

Poetry made nothing easier for Bug and Bug Spray as children, as heated-up teenagers hounding each other, and as beautifully impossible white-hot lovers, and, predictably, as husband and wife for over sixty years managing the Helltel in Cord, North Carolina, where their deceased parents resided in room 209.

Bunny called him The Mister. If you asked his name, he answered with an unself-conscious giggleswallow that he was The Mister Rounceval. Over time, no one recognized him by any other name.

Bunny could see no real harm had come to the young people. She had certainly not expected them here. She had imagined Acker trashing Room 202 (nope, clean), backing her toilet up (nope, neat commode), staining the ceilings with her vapething (nope, nope—strong, affecting mycophagous smell of vapecloud, but no stain). She had imagined one gun locker, not four lockers larger than she could have imagined. As far as she could tell, Acker was a good person and a strange person and probably not evil but possibly dangerous, extremely dangerous if something set her off.

The Mister Rounceval and Bunny had not imagined this poetry in Acker's bed, though Acker had told them, same as she told everyone in Cord and at the Helltel, that she was an International Performance-Artist-Writer and was Bad-Ass Famous and, in The Literary Bazaar, she was The Sorceress Acker and Her Eminence Acker and Acker Punk Legend, a brand as recognizable as Saran wrap.

When The Mister Rounceval returned with his favorite bush loppers, Bunny woke up the yinyang beetle-like thinghuman by touching the back of its head and/or buttocks, and loudly asking, "You uncomfortable?"

The metal scrape of the disengaging safety latch on the loppers claimed the full attention of Alice, who was close enough to Dookian's furry chute to actually taste her unfortunate situation.

She coughed, which made her belly feel the sticky slab of male bloat compressing her. Between her breasts, an inquisitive nodding thing. The way a—something—what?—a chicken neck would nod were it still attached to a chicken straining on the chopping block.

Her hair-trigger reflux response sent acid splash into her mouth.

The thing flopped, nodded, throbbed, an unsubtle, living, requesting thing, a seeking-bone. With a gristly spine or long tongue inside.

She could not lift her neck or head.

She could not raise her hips, her knees.

Cold, dead, living moving, head-twerking thing.

Tee-hee, she heard. Tee-hee.

Snake. The thing was snakelike.

A kind but warbled old voice, a woman's said, "Move most gently if move you must—"

"—in this lonely place," came the other voice, a man's, old, older than any Alice had ever heard.

Over each of her ankles, a swelling excruciatingly tight pastry. A large bullfrog. A not-dead gibletty gripper twitching over each of her ankles. Restless. She could not lift her head to look. She swallowed the cry that cinched her throat. Wet laughter came from inside that cry, from the source of all her cries all her life.

She needed to wipe her streaming sweat, the dribbling corners of her mouth. Impossible to reach or touch her face.

As far as she could tell she held small, canvas-covered bone-in roasts in her fingers. The sneakers of Dookian were taped firmly to her hands.

And her own small roasts. Her own canvas-covered feet and ankles. Taped inside his trembling insteps, which said, *Shitno. Shitno.*

Something was muttered into her pubis.

And it was shouted.

Motherfuck! Motherfuck! Dookian the Alice-surfer had no strength in any part of him except for his voice. Alice, ants and snakes and frogs upon her, could keenly feel his awareness of his body's weakness, his ridiculous struggle. She understood how a woman will dry up when she is a man's roast dish, how a man will go soft so fast when a bored woman's flesh withdraws beneath him.

Dookian was immobilized by his facedown position, but his voice came hard into her.

The old woman's voice asked, "You two always been such good friends?"

The old man patted the binding places. He gently cut Alice free from her man-size tumor.

The old woman said, "Heaven is here—"

"—where Juliet lives," said the man helping the angry Dookiantumor stagger to the bathroom.

Trying to remove the triple-tied small sneakers, Alice trembled, tears pouring from her eyes and nose. She lay again on the bed, which had no give to it.

A threadbare HH towel around his waist, the Dookiantumor wobbled on identical small sneakers through the flimsy open screen door to the balcony.

In a few seconds of time, the tumor's face had changed from livid to dazed to euphoric.

"Watch that one," said Bunny to The Mister Rounceval, who was now on the balcony with Dookian. They both understood Dookian might jump; his thighs were pressed against the low balcony rail, his chest was pitched forward, his hands reached out to hold nothing. The Mister was so close to him his chin nearly rested on the bulb of his shoulder, and he could see his trembling forearms and wrists. Union was near The Mister and the young Dookian, and he had a sense of inevitability about the young Dookian's hands. Because of long life, Union and The Mister both understood leaning out too far. Long life had given The Mister to understand leaning out too far because his mother and father, who had never been happy with having nothing, held him out before them into the promise of security and success, held their son out and over all the low railings in Cord. Dookian was smiling through nose-tears streaming down. Dookian's hands worried Union, who closely observed the loose and loosening grip of the hands on nothing.

And The Mister had a feeling about the hands, as well, about all young men's hands, all young parents' hands, about all the loosing that does not end after all the losing, and about the presence of Union who was, like him, not stopping young Dookian, his holding-on hands holding—holding only barely onto himself, barely holding onto the nothing that is the world's rickety, untrustworthy balcony.

"Watch that one!" Bunny repeated.

"Watch your own," said The Mister to Bunny.

"Will do."

Alice found she could not raise her knees or her shoulders or lift any part of herself free from the mattress where the side effect of the incident's hard medicine caused her teeth to chatter, her hands to jitter everywhere over her own naked body.

Sitting on the side of the bed, Bunny covered Alice up to her chin. Then—why not?—over her face.

And tightly tucked the sheet under the back of Alice's head.

Alice's moans were muffled better that way as Bunny stacked three pillows over her shrouded face, and plumped them and pushed down with determination, not long enough to do her in, but long enough to undo her more than she had ever been undone.

"What do you know about this, Child?" asked Bunny.

"Nothing," Alice said, unsure whether she had spoken or the word had echoed through her from Bunny's self-talk.

Bunny tried again, more precisely, "What do you know about this child?

"What? What child?" Bunny answered herself.

Alice could not make the words, so Bunny made them for her: "Nothing—what? What?"

Bunny spoke to herself, to Alice (who, it seemed, was inside Bunny), spoke aloud but from far inside herself and far away from Alice: "Dead, Child."

From underneath Dookian, The Mister Rounceval reached for the front of the towel around the young man's legs and, speedily pulling it back under Dookian's butt, he lifted it towards Dookian's upper back, and yanked abruptly in a hardy bucket-throw, and all of this done with very little difficulty. But with force.

"Do you smoke?" he asked the falling young man.

A young falling man does not hit the ground with a splash, nor with a bulb-breaking crushing noise. A falling young man jackknifes, his head tucking under a little, the flimsy cabinetwork of his shoulders taking the brunt of the impact, his hips then, then his legs fracturing in hundreds of hairline splinterings, his sneakered feet almost snapping off. A young man's landing body makes a screeching touching-down. From within him, a landing young man's bones beat every fiber of him like a well-thumped rug.

A young man hitting the ground from only two stories up, does not say "Oof!" or "God!" He seems, instead, to answer a question he has been asked about smoke. "No!" he says in the very private voice of an agent with no agency, of a noninvestigator at last investigating himself.

Union, of course, had been on the balcony all along. Listening to the howling storm of Bunny and The Mister Rounceval's grizzled laughter, he felt wonderfully uninterred from the burial place of his own storyteller's heart. This had happened to him many times: the discovery that the plot where you buried yourself is where you will dig or claw yourself out. If under the clay of your mind: your mind. If under your body: the clay of your body. If under your story-obsessed heart: the closed lid of your heart.

He thought, O, Dookian, you will survive, but roam this earth a ghost.

He thought, O, Young Alice, Mad Alice, what will keep slipping from its hidden place in you that you will wish would never, ever slip?

He thought, O, Rouncevals! If you stay in Cord for centuries you will never laugh so damn well, so damn long.

23.

Eddie said, "Sounds like two birds coming to the end of their warranties."

Eedie said, "Pretty as God on Her good days. Your ear's deaddead-deadheaded, Mister."

"No lie," said Eddie.

Jadia awoke to a swamp sparrow's squeaking call notes and dust-broom wingbeats entangled with Mrs. Panther's mocksinging and self-applauding. The secretkeeping light of the swamp circled inside dense maws of barbwire strategically placed and replaced in certain parts of the swamp over a one hundred year period; had you the courage to flee into the place of such scarifying sharkmouths, you could feel sure you and yours would not be taken away though you could be seen by bounty hunters who prowled the swamp edges and outermost canals.

As a child Jadia had been told about the Lumbee, the indigenous Americans in the swamps who intermarried into freedom and refused to be named anything but The People while very quietly preserving their always-evolving heritage. She learned about the Maroons who took refuge there in the seventeenth and eighteenth centuries. Her grandparents, who descended from escaped West Indies slave and Lumbee stock, told her all of this, and explained to her that she had come to be in Cord through her Maroon great-great-grandfather, recruited by the North to be a scout in 1864 and '65, in 1867 claim-ing a small parcel of land for farming long-staple cotton. He and his one-legged wife Yuga no sooner had their three children than he "passed on to glory 'thout passing on," they said, reserving the belief he might reside there still, a singing and sometimes a calling voice in the wetland reeds.

Mrs. Panther, flying under and over Webb, made a succession of sounds. She sounded like the locking and unlocking spirals of Lincoln's giant all-purpose high school notebook. She sounded exactly like him throwing shoulder pads and shin and arm guards into a gym bag with a long zipper closed with happy speed; sounded like his big bare feet tramping; like him loudly knocking around in the cereal and bread cupboard; like him rummaging in the fridge; toasting and overbuttering burnt toast; him picking up and putting down his phone device and when it hummed, humming back. She sounded like him wolfing cornbread, gulping milk, pouring more and gulping; sounded like him saying sadly to Acker, to Jadia, to Woolman, "No signal, no signal" during the thousand recovery commands when only silence came back from his Martian friend Oppy.

Like the millions of Oppynauts in nerdwarrens throughout the world, he and Woolman and Acker followed public access reports on the Red Planet dust storms deadly to Oppy, the "cleaning event" dust devils that might clear her solar arrays. The young men were attuned to the intensity of snare sound and top cymbal shimmer in Oppy's wavenet text-to-speech cosmic-female voice, the JPL assessments of her flash memory, the lulls in the storms within three thousand kilometers of her position, and the eerie silences persisting.

Because of the synchrony in hopeful young minds, the Oppynauts imagined barely audible whispersighs and noiseprimings, and a suggestion that these might be coming from their own bodies and their own devices generated new superpositioned silences. After Lincoln's death, the two lovers Woolman and Acker fixated so firmly on Oppy's silence that their sexual activities verged into more and more dangerous extremes of physical threat and injuring:

from their empathy grew a voracious need for revenging terrible silencings of truth.

Oppy had not responded to NASA's *Opportunity, Wake Up!* campaign, which developed into a massive Spotify playlist that included Billie Holiday's "I'll Be Seeing You" and Wham's "Wake Me Up Before You Go-Go" and "Telephone Line" by Electric Light Orchestra and Reed Kudzu Turchi's "Let It Roll" and Tom Petty's "I Won't Back Down" and the old Mississippi Fred McDowell song, "You Got to Move." Lincoln had simmered that McDowell song into new-school reggae that Acker and Woolman liked singing together.

Bits of the song now yelped through Mrs. Panther's version of Lincoln in his mother's kitchen, reminding her of Lincoln sounding like a washing machine thumping an unbalanced load: *You got to move. You got to move. You got to move, child, you got to move.*

Mrs. Panther bumped the notes and raked at the pauses in imitation of Lincoln practicing on his cornet, which was pretty permanently fixed to his Harmon mute. She sounded like the music coming—at all hours and at unimaginable volume—through his cheap earphones. She made the Lincolnsounds, the same ones as ever, the same old ones—she was sure they were the same ones—as on the night before Jadia walked out into the 2 a.m. darkness and found Lincoln murdered.

"Lincoln is not like the information with high teleportation fidelity," said Eedie.

"Not," said Eddie. "Not like that at all. Hard to retrieve."

"Dissolvable."

Jadia asked, "But you've seen Lincoln?"

"Here in this place right here and on this here branch." Eddie looked at the desiccated oak limb and at his fingerless hands planted there.

"Does he, you know, does he look bad—feel bad?" Jadia asked.

"Might be the wrong question."

She tried again, but not with speech.

"Dead doesn't feel worse. But it sure as hell looks worse to be dead before it looks better." Some connection between Eddie and the tree had come alive; he looked now at the upper limbs where something might have landed or taken off. "When you're through with the falling back out of yourself, with the sky coming up sudden on you, through with going up into—"

—"you're lighter—" said Eedie.

"—through with trickling down and dribbling off your bones—that's when you know—"

"—you're cloth dust, hair dust—" said Eedie.

"—bone dust."

"—a teaspoon of—"

"— dew or mud dew." Eddie looked at Eedie to know whether he should say more about the state in which your state dissolves but does not disappear. When Eedie gave him no indication, he said, "You start travelling then by evaporation. You evaporate into intersections like this place here, where you return and dispel and return."

"A long time passes before you're kicked out of one state into another," said Eedie. "You're seeds, you're a fist of seeds. Like milkweed or

117

dandelion or cotton fluff, and you don't have any say about how you dissipate and respirate and coexist with others. My Grandma Alcina came here and held me in her arms. She held me for the first time since she was dying, and she had died when I was seven, which was in the millionyears of vanishings after our first evaporations."

"Oh, Lord," said Jadia. "Lord, no."

"What are the odds? Some of the Alcina seeds flew here, some fell to I don't know where."

"But you two?" Jadia asked. "You're here?"

"We seem to be," said Eedie, unreliably. "I apologize, I do, Jadia. Eddie and I are contradictory information, aren't we?"

"Zat you?" Eddie asked the trunk of the tree as he discovered the vibrations from Union who was hiding inside.

Webb offered Union a useless warning bark. He wondered why no dog toy ever made a barking sound, why he was never given cough lozenges to help with overbarking. No life-size Jehovah's Witness chewable deliverance disciples. No dog lip gloss. No dog kneepads, no swimming goggles. He barked once more, less than pointlessly.

Union sighed. He understood his sighing would offer enough response to Eddie since he was no stranger to this intersection, this Passage where Eddie and Eedie had drowned during Hurricane Ophelia.

When Jadia heard the oak sighing, she laughed, convinced for a moment that she was under a dream spell inside a fairy tale.

Reading her, Eedie said, "We're not all here."

Eddie said, "You can see that, right?"

"But we're here, if you know what I mean." No sorrow marked Eedie's voice when she said, "This place is as real as real—like the intersection of 211 and 242."

Eddie said, "Lincoln came here. Alighted a few minutes. Said, 'My mother got here yet? Acker got here? Woolman? Any transmission from Oppy?' Wanted to know was he deaddreaming, and Eedie told him no, this was not one of the dream oaks. 'Will I be here again?' he asked, and we told him we didn't know yet if he was in the right state for that, which bummed him out, which made him ask if this place would ever be on his migration route. We told him he might come here again.

"He said, 'Well then—alright.'"

Jadia, who recognized her son's exact tone of voice, asked, "He said that? He said, 'Alright'?"

"Something like it," Eedie said. "You understand: we're reconstructing."

Jadia understood. Lincoln wasn't going to haunt the homes and churches and school classrooms and football fields and the consignment-bar and Acker's Helltel room or his mother's kitchen and living room. He wasn't a revenging spirit. He wasn't going to ghost the trailer park and the swing set where he was lynched.

Webb swallowed a tick he had snatched from his tail tip. He asked, How hard does a place have to hate on you for you to walk out—then forget you walked in—gave up falling-down tired—gave in to dreaming with two sucker limbs on a ghost oak—heard a sermon like every posthumansermon ever—something hard on your system as splintered chickenbones, spoiled vole meat, vulture shit. What, what is that, what is that—holy shit, ho-oh-oh-leeeeeeshit, what is that—Union you hear that? That's pretty big unchained

119

Dead—that's unafraid deepfreeze dead singing—you see that, you seen that—a lot like Dot in her floppy ruby slippers smelling the same as the first time I smelt her—her pluming toe scent shuffling in the hardwood. That can't be you, Dot—can't—what is that—what—you can't tell me—

Dot Nolo Doyle's muumuu billowed through a mudra of pine wreckage. Union recognized the particular pattern of the muumuu, and he felt his fear amplified by the billow-sound of her, and he said, "Webb, do something."

Me? Me? Webb barked.

Dot said, "I always liked you, Webb. And, Jadia dear, you—who do you have on your side now that your Lincoln's dead? Same people, I guess."

Jadia said, "What? Oh, Dot, that muumuu is beautiful on you."

Yeah, beautiful, really, Union said. Quiet down, would you, Webb?

Webb growled, Dot! That's Dot! You stupid? What? What if she's here to eat her weight in Webbsnack?

"That's unfair," said Dot. She unquietly, provocatively bared her teeth, said, "Don't be an unfairdog, little doggie." She barked at him, not a human pretending to bark like a dog, but the dog bark of a bitch-in-wet-heat pretending to be hungry-human.

Webb's spine flexed to the tail tip. He slurped at hot slobber.

"You're light in that one," Jadia said, not meaning anything about Dot's weight but, instead, about the beryl color of her muumuu, about her inlit magnitude. And Jadia thought about Lincoln, wishing her boy could have that form of lightness, wondering if he did or would.

Webb said, Jadia. Be careful—smell it? Smell what her tonguetip's giving off—smell how hungry she is?—is your smeller broke?

Union poured his thought into Jadia's: No! I won't let you. Webb won't let you. You have family to see to, and, anyway, people will come get you out of here, they'll drag you out and put you where you should be. If you stay for another day even, don't let it be with Dot. She's—

Dot said, "I'm on your side. You understand what I mean, don't you? I'll wait right here with you, Jadia. Together we'll wait for Lincoln." The slick scales of the swimming words "together" and "wait" glistened in the net of her speech.

"Are you always here?" Jadia asked.

"This is my trace," said Dot, not explaining that those who haunt a trace will track what should be found but will track down, as well, what should remain missing, and will never leave well enough alone.

This is not where you'll find him. Union wanted Jadia to understand. And tonight's moon is the wrong moon. He told Dot, Get your ass back to The Wherever.

"Careful, Union," said Dot, wagging her ass unseductively, doing her best eldritchy mutter. "I'll make your tasty bit of beast my bitch."

"Leave me—us—be," said Jadia. "I don't even much think about Cord or my people who I'll bet don't think about me longer than they did when I was underfoot. Is the Festival on?"

Full on, said Union. Fifth day.

"So Minister's already given his dumb sermon, flag been paraded around, a real feel-good time in town."

Webb growled, Mmmmhmm.

"The dog can stay," said Dot. "I got a pot your pet just fits."

Webb wondered how Dot's bones would sound if his teeth went down on them. He wished he had been read to as a pup or taught to read, taken out to the movies, had met spirits like Dot in the good wetfood and yeastwater of Lewis Carroll or Hans Vonnegut Anderson or in Aesop. They were names Union told him about. He could match them to story crumbs but not story loaves. So it goes.

Jadia said, "I'll rest here. You go on, Union. Dog, you lead that bird back to Cord." She was already easing to the ground, her knees and her hips landing, moved there by the fullness and fragility and the lifting and letting down in Dot's laughter.

She heard this world's lightest sail of sadness luffing in the swamp breeze, loudly emptying, making the travelling-on sounds.

24.

Mrs. Panther and Webb were gone. Union, who could linger at one of time's passages while entering or leaving another, had left her, Jadia supposed.

"Union," she said, "if you're there, don't be. Okay?"

Oh, came the echo word, and then came the echo-question from Union who had left and had remained: Eh?

The humid air—no breeze of any kind—dampened her skin. "I need to be alone now."

Oh.

"Dot?" she asked. "Eedie? Eddie?"

No answer came.

Jadia had not consciously chosen to abandon her friends, her community of Cord, her church. She had meant to step away but not to stay away for long. Under the spell of Dot and Eedie and Eddie, she felt, as never before, the world's promised calmness more apparent beneath veils of moss and vine and fallen leaves of hope, the calmness behind converging tendrils of mist and interlocking tree skeletons and bush limbs, the swamp's reciprocating calmness, the wheel inside the wheel. Sunlight and shade dodged on the watery surfaces in the spilling afternoon light. The longer she gazed, the more her eyes took in zones of color that she could touch and smell and hear and taste as words no one had taught her.

By late evening, the bellowing of frogs and the creaking and groaning of the oldest trees were indistinguishable inside one harmonizing choir-roar of Presences.

The last light blinked out.

"Union?" she asked. "Gone yet?"

He liked feeling her voice pass through him instead of resonating as it would against a surface less permeable. The word "gone" murmured at the base of his spine and expanded the dome of his diaphragm, the sound vibrating upward, becoming a releasing sigh from his own lips: Gone.

The situation made them both laugh, acknowledging that, of course, he could be where he was and, at the same time, somewhere else; he could be when he was and somewhen else at the timesame. "A haint is—and ain't" is the explanation you'd be given if somewhy you asked "How?" in the Appalachia you conceived but couldn't begin to perceive.

An ancient, brute wind moved through the swamp's dense and sparse realms of forest and forest ruins, a passing blow before a strike.

"Turn around now, Union—I gotta get out of this old thing."

Eh?

"Turn around."

She pulled her long shift dress over her shoulders, looking down at the empty waist and arms and collar, at the white stripes on the gray. She shook out the thin cotton, which billowed, huffed, gulped. The forest floor hummed in the instant before the next gusting windblast lifted her arms over her head, and when she brought them back down, more air caught in the cloth.

She planted her feet, flexed her knees, bent her upper body over, surprised when that movement pivoted her directly into the strong wind's obliging hands.

A somersaulting launch gently placed her in the closest pendant branch above her head.

A bed of warm air under her, a coverlet of warmer air over her, she slept.

25.

Low-level state investigators, a team of three young men named Melvin, Shaw, and Ward, checked into the Helltel on the sixth day of the Festival. Oil in their hair, uncalloused hands nervously closed, slim black-leather folders under their weak wings: the three white boys looked newly hatched from their white NC-state vehicle.

Studying them through the front window of the consignment-bar, Acker asked, as if inside the minds of these three young ducklings, as if in her authorial mode of cold rage, "Where to start?

"One: Agent Dookian humpty-dumptied from a great fall, off in a Wilmington hospital.

"Two: Agent Alice, still here, mad-hatter-mad more or less.

"Three: Town under the spell of a beast.

"Four: A lynching murder covered up.

"Five: A phantasmic missing person in the swamp.

"Six: Machete-wielding Panther on the loose.

"Seven, eight, nine, ten, eleven, twelve through fourteen: haunted old hotel, burning swing set incidents, Oppy crisis, fiddle music, funnel-cake-vomit smell, some kind of gun-worshipping-veteran-honoring music festival, local, annual, hard to tell, three white boyagents touch down unannounced. Should I google that, should I forward that to official hindquarters?"

Yes, google away, said Union, nudging the one shared shoulder of the Pine family, setting their smooth pine heads rocking affirmatively forward and back. Young Pine had been reglued to his family. The glue had been thickly applied at Young Pine's throat, and the result was a shining dickey.

Woolman and Junior Stanley smiled at each other because they might have heard Union Vedder but couldn't be certain.

Junior and Minister were upright citizens of Cord and were outwardly honorable men who had helped the festival stay on its wobbling feet through the years, who had kept the consignment-bar going through many downward cycles, who had a sound relationship in which they looked out for each other. Both had voted Obama and both had voted Trump, and their decisions could be simply explained the same honest, sincere way: everyone they knew was voting like that.

The two men were actually humble, not praise-me-I'm-humble, not I-can-do-humble-better-than-you. They were nothing like Lisbet had been when she was part of the family: she dared to think her own thoughts, to feel what she herself felt, to listen to others and deep within herself to carry the voice of the crowd in her consciousness without being carried by it away from deeper self-reckonings of conscience. Her mother Orelia had never felt permission to be anything like Lisbet or like Minister Stanley or Junior Stanley: she knew she was supposed to wear a covering of invisibility and deference from head to toe. Her forbearing was supposed to show her noble manner and reinforce for others the grace of the veiled life.

When Lisbet died Orelia had no daughter who would lift the veil and ask, Mother, will you let me know you and fight with what you are and let me find my true nature in the fight with all your choices?

Neither Minister nor Junior could be dared by Lisbet to live in courageous daring.

Acker said, "Three little ducklings, Ward and Shaw and Melvin, three little-dick detectives, Melvinwardandshaw, here to solve the case, Shawardandmelvin, Melvandshawarden here to look us over. If they were an agency and had agency, wouldn't that be absolutely bloominduckloverly? And never in their lives have they seen so many saltines." Acker, who was naturally synonymic, found the word "Cracker" insufficient.

Almost eight hundred people had come from the outlying communities to attend the 2017 Soldier's Joy Festival claiming all eight blocks of Cord. At one end of the aisle of thirty-two booths was a stage for the fiddle playing and singing performances and competitions. At the other end stood a gaudy canary-yellow circus Information & Ticketing tent caricaturizing the design of the old Rosenwald schoolhouses. The tent was emblazoned with the words Welcome Home USNRA.

From the tentskin the open eyes of giant trompe l'oeil windowpanes shone, uncannily reminiscent of the book depository windows popular with tourists visiting Dallas, Texas.

Cord's first festival of any kind occurred in 1959. It had been called The Beast Festival because of the legend of an elusive creature terrifying the town and the nearby communities of Worthy and Ninepin and Decker and Meet, beginning in winter of 1957. The thing we feared stalked us, found us, tore apart the bodies of our goats and chickens, our roasting-age pigs, our pet dogs and cats and some of our old, abused horses, and even the rafters hereabouts of elusive wild turkeys roaming the land's shadowy, folded places like retired preachers.

At night, always at night, the beast stalked our weakest: the elderly and the children and grandchildren and great-grandchildren, who were too frightened to report consistent or even vaguely accurate sighting stories but who told sighting stories nevertheless.

We did not wait to learn more about this beast.

In our region of drowsy Presences we do not have to wait to discern whether the shadow creature before us is ours, is us. We have guns.

We have guns that we gently lift into and out of their cleaning cradles, our instincts brought alive by the smell of steel chambers and barrels, by the taste of lubricant, of degreaser, our skin yielding to the weapon's polished skin, our muscles responding to the heft of the stock, the pulse in our fingers and palms when they are upon the gun grip and the trigger release.

We stalked the beast so successfully that in an eighteen-month period our local and state papers featured half a dozen beasts hung on meat hooks on different porches, the great white hunters in the standard heroic poses, the hunters' stories, the admiring reactions of local and state officials in pre-election heat.

We do not mock redundant killing, not in Cord.

We have guns.

After the beast was killed, there were fewer incidences for a period of time, then none, and then increased sightings unreliable, reliable, irrefutable, before, eventually: The Return of the Beast.

In those first years of being shadowed by our shadow, we speculated about the beast as a Biblical scourge. After 2008 we understood the beast was God's just repayment for homosexuality, for femiliberal Pelosis, for Jew-Schumers and dark Ricers and Lynches and Holders and Baracks and Michelles and Billhillaries controlling everygoddamnthing, for immoral grown white women and young white women, for iniquitous, pregnable, promiscuous female illegals, for Muslim brotherhoods butting into our brotherhoods, for terrorist-foreigners and enviromaniacs cutting in line for and cutting out our jobs, for families failing in their faith duties. We go to our knees for no man; we stay on our knees for PC, the Prosperity Christ, who only asks of us that we have fear of God and have money to mail in. We born-again consumers have a full understanding of God's ferocious appetite for our God-fear. We have elemental fear you will never pry from our cold, dead hearts.

Red-lined verse and chapter, we have learned to pray in the name of the fatherfear and the fearother and the fearafter. We, a chosen Christian nation, are fear's ministers, fear's minister's cowed daughters and cowherd sons. Fire, crosses, robes. Rope. Ruination. Threat of torture, threat of beatings, threat of maimings. Rape. And guns.

We have faith in guns. During the hunting of the dark beast, the rear entrance to a one-room Blackfolks' church was riddled with bullets. A fire, set to flush the beast from hiding, burned the picnic shelter at AME Baptism Pond.

A middle school student lost her hand and forearm in friendly gunfire during a beast hunt the *Constitution Times* reported October 1, 1958, as "almost successful." A first grade school picture of the maimed Black child made the front page; the accompanying article did not name the father-and-son team of shooters. The newspapers did not acknowledge that the beast exclusively stalked white people and white people's family members and animals and properties.

The Beast story repeatedly made the national news as an entertaining myth, and The Beast Festival had sprung up more or less as our celebration of finally being on the map.

For a time, the festival grew in size and in friendliness and in good weirdness. Many kinds of dark Brillo-haired beast likenesses on T-shirts and many kinds of child-appropriate, cuddly, stuffed, velvet-black beasts and many barbecue beast sauces and sweet baked-beast goods and fresh beast sandwiches: people, Black and white alike, could find humor in all our self-deprecating ways of monetizing our ridiculous efforts to kill fear, and, failing, to own and unleash that fever in our flesh. The Church of the Word sold homemade canned chow-chow, six dollars and sixty-six cents a jar. *Scary Good*, the label said in English. And in Portuguese, *America Assustador*.

Every year, our church councils, with half as many extended white families attending church services as in the past, blocked the participation of gun manufacturers until low-level executives would agree to extortion money called "Samaritan funding," an idea we borrowed from the con-minister Franklin Graham, the heart-deformed issue of the famous brand name, Billy Graham.

It goes without saying that gun manufacturers Samaritanized possible losses by offering "essential continuing community support" to relevant county commissions in annual closed sessions that, by law, should have been open to the public. From 1981 to 2001 the event, retaining the essence of absurd beastiness, became The Bushmaster Festival.

In 2002 the organizations Ghost Guns and Ghost Gunner co-sponsored a profitable festival booth called *Mister Scratch* that sold two kinds of machines for gunsmithing. Expensive machines. No questions asked, *Mister Scratch* sold parts kits, and firearm receivers, and printed and online instruction manuals for homemade production of weapons, including assault weapons. The unregistered and untraceable ghost guns infuriated the Bureau of Alcohol, Tobacco, Firearms and Explosives, and that fact made the weapons especially appealing to us all.

At the first moment of ghost gun market significance, the local NRA chapter promptly took over the festival's "increasingly challenging administrative responsibilities," and excluded *Mister Scratch* and all other ghost gun hobbyist trade from participating in the festival.

According to the NRA's usual protocols, an aggressive public relations campaign seeded our community with misinformation, beginning in 1981. In the first plantings, the NRA conflated lawful possession with freedom, existing legislation with absolute right, home protection with border security. The NRA made happy fools of our people who liked the boom in bullet sales that they imagined as the sound of dog whistles, and who, at that time anyway, knew damn well the difference between demagogic ideas and democratic ideals.

In the next NRA plantings, the code term "Southern culture" was unsubtly applied to gun clubs, gun lore, even to inheritances of gun cabinets and gun collections. The smallest of these propaganda efforts echoed loudly as they penetrated the poorly boarded-up mines of old beliefs about "the Northern war of aggression."

The NRA then linked supporting the troops with the Second Amendment rights of patriotic veterans who had, after all, protected us from "Islamic domination." Veterans, who were real-life heroes in their home communities, became paid NRA consultants.

Rumors were circulated about diminishing ammunition supplies. Complicit local gun-store owners, who knew the manufacturers increased ammunition costs according to the success of these rumors, appreciated the realization of each prophecy of increased profit, and they secretly called their scamgame Revelation—in some cases, Revelation 22:22 for the Bible verse that does not, in fact, follow the twenty-first final verse.

These efforts took many years. Once people would eat the poison those plantings yielded, they would lap up the steaming Foxshit that Barack Hussein Obama was the great emasculator of the USA, which had been the world's preemptive murderous bully during the glorious Junior Bush era; they would accept that Obama had a grand plan to break into our homes and our hunting clubs to destroy our gun supply chains, to confiscate our ammunition, and to take away all guns, everfucking one, to then lock up all male, white former gun owners in a special federal maximum-security prison, a massive but top secret, totally inaccessible rendition facility thought to be located somewhere in Maine or Vermont or Massachusetts.

The main hobby of most folks here, men and women, young and old, turned with breakneck speed from time-honored civic and familial hunting traditions to blind stockpiling of human-killing military-grade weapons. The name—the actual name—of the elderly presence who led the four decades of focused NRA efforts to undermine hundreds of years of proud gun-skills traditions here was Craven A. Mercer, related in essence to the famous Mercers, though not in DNA.

If Union Vedder had manufactured a name like that only for the spirit of a story, all of Cord would firmly correct him; if Union changed that actual name to something more credible, he would have been condemned by every local who ever paid him any attention; if Union pointed out that North Carolina had a county named Craven, he would have been told that was fake news.

The obscenely wealthy Craven A. Mercer had a sister named Gyldan. That seems preposterous unless what you believe is that every human path is predestined.

Naming matters to us. "You did not choose me, but I chose you," so says John's Gospel.

The Bushmaster Festival was never on the scale of the convention center gun shows in other southern cities and towns, but it had a special appeal to buyers avoiding the closer gun regulation scrutiny that might occur in those places. The local NRA chapter felt that none of the appeal to gun-hoarders was compromised when Junior Stanley, co-chair of the festival committee, suggested the new name,

The Soldier's Joy Festival, ostensibly a tribute to the fallen soldiers Eddie Carter Lang and Aaeedah Willerton Clodd.

In the last years of the Obama era and the first year of the Trump Reich the event became a stronger-than-ever rallying center for white supremacy organizations, extreme fundamentalist church groups like Church of the Word, militias, and militia recruiters. These organizations did not just spring up. They had grown here, of course, through many plantings meant to smother the little failed democracies planted by grandmothers and grandfathers, mothers and fathers, sisters and brothers; planted by lovers and exes, believers and disbelievers, laborers and bosses, givers and grifters; planted by neighbors distant and near; planted by leaders with skins of different colors.

Isolating selfishness and brainlessness and falseness and cultic madness grew in the lightless church of narcissism that Cord became. Unbearable aloneness and helplessness and truth-hunger and paradoxical terror of the truth rose up inside the dark, and roamed. And feasted.

The locals, who made and served the festival food, who arranged the wonderful musical entertainment that included our own talented, beloved children and teenagers, benefited from the annual occasion, the reminder of and the escape from the sorrows in our country's abandonment of community and kinship, a decades-long process of decay having its date of origin on January 20, 1981. Since there are no adults now, there will soon be no adult relationships, no illuminating adult engagements reaching beneath the surface for linkage, communication, tolerance. There will soon be no adult desire for fulfilling peace among us, no singular expression of loving-kindness toward one beloved familiar or unfamiliar beloved one. There will be, essentially, no *us* in Cord.

"No one to shout the difference between then and now. No one to tell us what time of night it is," wrote a pioneer American prophet, her name forgotten in the Blue America, obliterated in the Red.

We brought out-of-town friends to attend the boisterous, celebratory extravaganza, the outward embodiment of Southern graciousness and unpretentious good-neighborliness. We brought friends who felt judged in other places and under other circumstances, who approved of themselves and who appreciated being among other self-approving folk.

We advertised the romantic joys of soldiering, of preparing for hardship and of soldiering on through fear, of training to cause death and to die, of celebrating the victims of and the survivors of soldiering.

We sold.

We sold.

We mastered selling. The festival visitors here felt like the sightseers one hundred and fifty years ago who had traveled to the bluffs above Lee's Ferry in order to picnic and to imbibe while they enjoyed observing the first killing shots fired in the conflict that would become the Civil War.

26.

"Did you see them?" asked Minister. He and Junior pointed to the faintly illuminated blue marbles in clusters on the bar ceiling of Stanley'sAcker'sStanley's.

"Now that's—" To give Acker a closer look, Junior turned the bar-room lights on, showing her the marbles brought by Drummer were not manufactured lightbulbs. "That's—"

Minister said, "They came like that."

Union felt the tearing of the frail tissues existing between overworld and world. The betweenness of this mineral-light called to mind eon-echoes of *Beware. Beware.*

"That's phantasmic," said Acker as an odd warning spoken to Minister and Junior. Phantasmic. As in, Don't fuck with this dark magic—I love you two as much as I love my BDSM-Barbie, but I don't trust you with this. She felt she recognized the marbles, their strange false color from the same band combination generated by the browse tool, Worldview.

Junior would not believe in the existence of them as anything but a trick. He knew his father would see the marbles as a sign of something to believe in, and while Junior could believe blindly and stupidly in ordinary horror, he could not and would not believe in wonder.

Acker said, "Lincoln. He's done this. Am I right, Mike?"

Mike, prominent but reticent Ackerpatch, gave no answer.

"He brought this." She used her device's camera to harvest several images of the ceiling crop. "This what I think it is, Siri?"

"Sorry. You said?"

"Siri, don't fuck with me, you little algozoa. This is hematite: confirm for me if you can—hematite?"

"Let me see. Touring. Touring.

"Touring.

"Touring."

"Her Siri gives me the willies," said Junior to Minister.

"Not exactly harmful though, is she?" said Minister. Minister did not say what he thought: that Junior was *misborn*. Junior's vulnerable fearfulness and his willingness to betray his own values on a moment's notice in order to feel safe; Junior's superficiality and his get-along-to-go-along shape-shifting, which allowed him to be sincere and gracious and invisibly pernicious and false; Junior's readiness to help anyone in need as long as his own needs would be paramount in the bargain. Minister and Orelia had never meant to give birth to this: a man who called himself a Prayer Patriot and a Proud Boy and told them he was part of a kind of treehouse club of Proud Home Guard Boys. They had no idea how to understand: he was a grown man who ought to have learned some humility, but he was part of a group that wanted to brag it was proud? Proud of what? Junior apparently wanted to be among men who would act like little boys by talking tough to others, boys so immature they imitated each other's faux-militaristic ways of speaking? And they thought that dressing alike and talking in the same babyboy ways and posing for wanna-be-badboy pictures was patriotic. What? And looking at him, a man they loved who had devolved to a boy proud of being among other boybabyposers, Minister knew that what he and Orelia wished to see born in the world was gone.

Siri said, "Download complete. The image illustrates hematite. Found on Mars, Meridiani Planum, also Utah, southern region, Moqui National Park located in—"

"*Enough.* Jesus!"

"Touring. Touring. Shall I continue?"

"Bye now."

"Good," said Siri, and, after an abnormal pause, "Bye."

Junior said, "This makes no sense. You think you've seen this kind of thing before?"

Acker said, "Don't worry about this, Junior. This is a little gift from Lincoln. He's showing us. He's showing us Mars close-up and personal."

"Mars." Minister, who had heard many times from Lincoln and Woolman about Oppy, the Mars rover, liked the idea of the charged mind creating the perfect ground for lightning, which he had once believed was not at all different from hearing the Lord and receiving the laying on of His hands through the electric hands of the preacher. How long had he believed that what his own mind created it owed to a Creator?

"I don't like it," said Junior. "Mars?"

Acker said, "I'll explain later. It's showtime for me at the festival."

She left in order to follow the three young investigators as they walked out of the Helltel and into the festival crowd. The alert investigators held selfie sticks at their sides so they could shoot groupface portraits of meta-togetherness in good late-afternoon light. They also shot their individual fablefaces foregrounded in a context of apartness from everything going on around or behind them or within them. They constantly adjusted the glinting selfie cobra heads held above them.

Sometimes the young investigators opened their mouths tongue-back teeth-out as they shot a future-perfect-continuous photo-semblance. Sometimes they extended their wands to maximum length and lifted them high in order to achieve app-omnisciences, high-def artsy images of the festival herd that could later be reality-enhanced. The young simulacra would later curate imaginings of themselves with images in which they will have been celebrating what will have been culminating in that moment of resembling themfutureselves expiring.

Acker was accompanied by two handsome handguns in an old-fashioned leather shoulder holster, and Mrs. Panther and Mr. Panther were on either side of her.

Mrs. Panther's singing mocked the fiddle music arguing with the Latin beat of powdered sugar shaken over funnel cakes. *Ye-ha! Ye-ha!* she sang, mocking the Word of Godders standing where they could break the flow of festivalgoers in order to preach their enigmatic four-word sermon, "Ye have prayed it." Mrs. Panther mocked the increasingly strong wind making a firm *nope* sound on the walls of the small and large festival tents. She mocked the sales pitches: *"Beast Leg deep-fried! Teriyaki keeeeeeebab! Corn Dog! Hawt Pretzel! Hawt Pretzel! BeastBQ!"*

27.

At the consignment-bar Junior couldn't be sure of his feeling that the ceiling formations, whatever they were, were spreading. "How?" he asked.

"Some kind of magician's illusion is my guess." Minister lifted his open hand toward a cluster of the small round minerals, which caused them to float down almost to his fingertips. "I wonder. This could be like a palming trick, like The Great Tomsoni. Your mother and I saw him perform once in a Raleigh bowling alley. He could turn his hand a certain way and spray a million leaves, real leaves, over a crowd in a small room or a big stage. And no trees anywhere to be seen." Dead now, thought Minister—with honest doubt.

"Who brought them in?" asked Junior.

"Your mind brings them. That's what kind of mind God gives his people: easy to trick."

Truer words were never spoken, thought Union, who also remembered The Great Tomsoni and his assistwife Pamela Hayes. She was always equally engaged in working the crowd and upending its next-second expectations, no one referring to her as great.

"Seriously. Who brought them here?"

"Drummer brought them. Yesterday. In satchels. Turn the room lights back off so you can see them better."

"Trade?"

"Traded them for three of Mrs. Labboard's methdolls." Minister had not liked the toddler-size raggedy sisters, hand and foot amputees poorly sewn together from yellowed muslin, stuffed full with cotton lint that bulged from the eyes and mouths ripped into leers and smiles with an unsharpened knife and sloppily resewn. Mrs. Labboard made BB-stuffed dolls, as well, and Dot and Orelia and Marie and Bunny and others had their own original little Labboard methdolls, their own beloved, shockingly impaired doll companions.

When Junior flipped the wall switch, the blue hematites disappeared. He flipped the switch back on. At a nod from Minister, he floated some down to him, looked closely, floated them back up with the same teacup-lifting gesture. He tested their responsiveness by blowing lightly upward, which made them briefly swell. He breathed in. "Imagine!" he said, resisting imagining.

"Tomsoni played bass harmonica for us. Pamela Hayes—our Festival secretary, you know—lives in the Helltel—brought a boy up to the stage, and Tomsoni palmed that boy's hair, then all our hair—a hundred or more of us—well, it stood on end—and Pamela's, too, so her hair was three feet over her head. That boy's hair stayed just like it had been. Tomsoni played 'How Do You Keep the Music Playing?' and made every note a sour one but beautiful—try that kind of musical magic if you think you can."

"Dad," Junior said. "Dad."

"Acker's not going to want to let these marbles go." She was a hoarder of anything she called phantasmic, and Minister had often argued with Acker about "letting *everything* that comes in go out for the right price," which she called "Moneycrazy" and he called "Profit Motive Philosophy 101."

The ceiling marbles waltzed when Minister right-circled-left-circled-left-circled his arms above his head. They perched in his hands and upon his shoulders. Clacked on the ceiling, tapped on and bounced from the floor. They responded to him by rattling against each other. If he moved his hips, they hopped at his waist. They *learned*, and, like all learners, they taught: touch with the heat of your mind.

"You say Drummer brought them?"

Minister answered, "There weren't so many, Son. A dozen. You think she knew they were going to reproduce?"

"Who in heaven would buy them?"

The question made Minister ashamed of his own diminished talents. He felt he no longer had his salesman's instincts for selling goods or God to man or woman. "I could get someone to trade for them," he said, but said, "no, I couldn't—who am I trying to fool?"

Junior's amused, loving, middle-school grin was a reminder to Minister of how one kind of happiness could be traded for another with no money exchanged. You're a good-probably-good son and misborn, he thought, and unselfish in a showy way, and selfish as Adam on Day One. Minister had a passing vision of a new consignment-bar sign: ~~Stanley's~~~~Acker's~~~~Stanley's~~Proud Boy Junior's.

"You have to see this," said Junior to Woolman and Jacob, who sat near the bar and who seemed not to have noticed at all the change in atmosphere, the wet-clay odor, the rising and lowering ceiling blueberries, the increasing sense of bursting release.

Minister asked, "Do you think this has a name? I mean, is there a word for this?"

"Shit, that's some strangeness there," said Woolman but in a tone of relative responsiveness that gave Junior and Minister no satisfaction.

Not shifting one grain of his focus upon Woolman, Jacob said, "Don't God work in mysterious ways."

Junior set his red hat back on his head so he could watch the rock marbles configure and reconfigure. He didn't like this, any of it. Why did Cord give people like Acker a place at the table? Who gave permission for anything to be different ever than the way it had been?

Laughter came from the deepest inner caves of Minister. "This is. Not. *These*. These are not God's usual devices."

28.

"I'll be seeing you fuckers."

A

The five words of Acker's suicide note were stickied to the bar fridge. Woolman and Jacob found it there, and because they did not assume the worst, they stayed on their barstools, ignored Minister and Junior and the mesmerizing ceiling, a kind of inverted pool table with none of the balls yet pocketed.

Jacob carved away mold on a greasy summer sausage, and he handed his son thick pieces, and Woolman pushed the beer bottle toward Jacob who served himself, poured for Woolman, and they hesitated to acknowledge each other but sometimes glanced, sometimes looked, and their anticipation about Skyping with Marie in an hour was the cause of reflux burping for them both, Jacob unselfconsciously swiping back the cowlick on his left temple, Woolman sausage-greasing the hair on his own head in a gesture identical to Jacob's. Woolman wondered whether Acker's note meant "you fuckers" or "you, fuckers," whether or not tonally her note argued "I'll *be* seeing you fuckers" or "I'll be *seeing* you, fuckers," but he did not check it again, and Jacob who had heard for all of his life what he called "the visitor voices" now heard Acker splash acidly inside Woolman, and he understood she had loved Lincoln, loved him truly, loved Woolman no less, and he knew Acker had no use for the usual rules concerning romantic notions of possessor and possessed.

"Did you know what Lincoln wanted to be?" asked Woolman.

Jacob had no way of knowing. And the question of wanting to be this or that profession had always been more than a little confounding to the tinker-saunterer who only knew he wanted to repair things that were simple to repair, and he wanted to talk at length with and hear gossip from his customers. Jacob said, "He had plans?"

"Yeah." Lincoln had figured how his college schedule would be set up, had nailed down a part-time job in Raleigh, his mother listening to his plans, remaining silent as he described them. He told her that if everything fell in place he would be pre-law. His real intention was to be a planetary geologist. He had told only Acker and Woolman that particular secret, since he could not imagine anyone but them understanding.

Jacob asked, "What does a planetary geologist do? What was he really going to be?"

Woolman thought, He was going to be happy. Really. He was going to leave Cord happy, grow his happiness, become a planetary geologist, a happy one. He said, "It was a secret he asked me to keep, and I should have kept it."

"Well, I understand about keeping secrets."

"I guess you do."

Wanting to shift their conversation, Jacob said, "This is a good sign—that your mother wants to appear—to, you know—"

"Skype."

"She's trying to break through. I wish she would just talk to us, that would be better, but the Skype-place is where she figures she can do this, I guess." He asked Woolman, "Do people believe the Skype-place is real?" Like every Cordite, Jacob knew about The Passages, the places where the weave loosens over the hidden world wearing this world as disguise.

145

"It *is* real."

"Could be."

"What's with this 'Could be'? You've been there with me and Mom. We've been there, and we're going there again, and we can go there all we want. It's a technology. It's a tool."

"Could be." Together, Jacob and Woolman now observed the swelling Martian blueberries letting down enough to further darken the room of the bar. Though NASA geologists had named them "blueberries" they looked more like stoneberries, like dark-magic food in a fable.

They listened to the afternoon fiddle competition. They listened to pistols firing, the silence after the explosions. Mufflers, they guessed. It made no sense that the sound would be coming from pistols.

They stopped pouring and instead they swigged the beer. They carved sausage pieces. Had there been napkins they would have ignored them.

Without shifting his gaze from this toxic world's threatening generosity, Jacob asked, "She scare you?"

"She's scary."

"Amen. Always has been."

"Amen."

In a matter of months, Jacob and Woolman had resistantly and then happily crossed from being estranged familiars to being family-strange.

They talked in the way a young man and an older man in nine feet of darkness will who are digging farther down, leaving the most crucial talking to the shovels.

29.

Acker had made no dramatic announcement to the Soldier's Joy Festival crowd when she used a Smith & Wesson Shorty .40 in each hand to achieve maximum deadly effect for the self-inflicted gut shots that almost bisected her.

Mr. Panther assisted the new young investigators who put Acker's body on ice in the bathtub of a first-floor room at the Helltel. He noticed that the blood spatter was honeycomb gold, and that the thick layers of white powder always coating her face were crazed as if by a kiln fire. He asked the dead Acker aloud, "Acker. Hey, Acker. Tell me. What *are* you?"

"The fuck?" said agent Melvin.

Mr. Panther said, "You should be more careful."

"We got this, old man," said agent Shaw.

"She your friend?" asked agent Melvin.

"You could say that," he answered. "She's like a sister."

Agent Shaw didn't care what this old Black fellow was to this dead woman. He said, "Sure."

Mr. Panther said, "I don't know what I mean by that."

The three young investigators Ward, Shaw, and Melvin, were surprised at how easily they could lift and move her and position her in the tub, but they did not consider whether she had been more diminutive than she appeared. The handguns, which they did not remove from her hands, felt as heavy as she. Blood had streamed down over her branching red leg tattoos and into her boots, which had weight greater than her hips or legs or feet. The multiple separate wound channels of the expanding bullets had caused her body to try shedding her yarn-threaded neckskin, but had only shrugged it down; her tongue projected far from her blackened mouth, and her pink rubber-tipped stud and the middle groove of tongue muscle were glazed with syrupy bile. The same bile brimmed in her open, bulging eyes, splashed from her lower lids onto her cheeks.

The Acker body was gone from the bloody tub when the coroner arrived two hours later.

30.

On the evening of the festival's sixth day, the Acker body returned to Stanley's-Acker'sStanley's in one of Dot's muumuus, a PeterMaxish color-spilling design of open hands falling out of open hands flying out of half-closed hands flinging out of bare fists, and all of that against a background of nuclear Japanese-Shinto-motif winter. The platinum roots of the body's black hair were whiter and her black lipstick blacker. The white face makeup whiter. Looking under the muumuu, Webb observed that more branches of tattooed red streamed down the body's slender legs. Except for the belly pouch that included bloodstained Mike, the outfit was not the body's usual.

Woolman, who had been brought a short while earlier to see the corpse in the icebath, burst into tears at the sight of her standing behind the consignment cash register, and he stammered, "You're —you're—beautiful in that thing—*jesusjesus*—you scared me out of my fucking mind, Acker, all of us thought you were deadgone for sure."

Webb, at Woolman's feet, took a closer look, closer smell, deeper smell of what was missing and what was only added now. He wished the Acker body was wearing Dot's muumuu with the famous-fountains design: he could clean his coat by looking at Dot's fountain spray; he could bathe his tongue in her puddles, clear his sinuses with that odor of drycleaning solvent on the fabric. You brought me something from the regions of the dead? he wanted to ask the Acker body.

Union said, Fool dog.

Webb growled. Good to have fresh-killed—fresh-killed is best.

Jacob said, "That was not funny, Miss Acker. Whatever you think, you shouldn't have done that."

"Hmm," the Acker body said, lifting its arms over its head and trembling them down to its sides. "Died?" The body released Prom vapor.

"Yes, young woman. Died. Woolman passed out, hit the floor and couldn't get himself up. I thought he'd had a heart attack or something."

"Oh, Woolman," the body said, "Always overreacting to violent, meaningless death."

"You were on ice," Woolman said.

"All my life," said the body. "Am I right, Siri?"

"So right!" said Siri in her best Señor Wences ventriloquip.

Because the right dose at the right moment always helped, the body debbed hard, *Vvew*!

"Hee-hee," said Siri, a technological construct less than ten years old, a deathless consciousness.

"Thank you, Pedro," said the body.

The body coughed, opened the cash register where Union stood, flipped up one of the bill compartments, did the expected Dire Straits mimic, "Moneyfernothin."

Woolman smiled. That one always got him, every single time, though the musical allusion was lost on him, on his generation of gleety hiphopster-mixmashering-trancedancer-rockhaters.

"A little suicide effort. Not my first bad ending. A little UBH." The body's voice was hoarse-whispery, like a lazy elderly elevator, like a train gaining velocity. Who knows the transubstantiating hotel floors and switchyards a voice has traveled to when it sounds like that?

Jacob, Woolman, Minister Stanley, Stanley Junior, Webb, and Union took a long look at the Acker body in the colorful muudrapery, more than ever a surprising body rippling somberly but brightly and vibrantly against its own clay banks. Not the body of the unhappy dead.

Invisibly present inside Acker's debtide, Union thought, Shouldn't toes peek out at the bottom of that muumuu? Shouldn't her muumuu be less transparent? Shouldn't a body that has returned from the dead put on underclothes, have less vapetude? Shouldn't a body brush the traces of blood from its teeth and lips and chin and hairline? Shouldn't a body wear the usual overdose of men's cologne?

Webb smelled his penis, a nervous habit he could not shake. The half-stiff loaf smelled ovenfresh. He wondered—he felt self-conscious, since he heard Union's disapproving sigh, and so, of course, he wondered: What honest penis owner, lugging his fragrant gift everywhere he went, would go sniffless?

Minister Stanley said, "What God asks …" but without God's assistance could not find the wick in the sentence's wax.

"Huh?" his son said.

Webb said aloud, "Nothing is more real than nothing," sure that no one heard. A long-ago companion schnauzer, Mr. M, had told him that, a strapping hunter and digger who had died toothless, tepid.

The sight of the body had shocked Minister Stanley. He called to mind the seven magical words, "I am the resurrection and the life." That was God's habit as a Vegas-type magician: to fully manifest finality and infinite renewability. God, after all, had taken his young daughter Lisbet from Orelia and from him and from Cord and from the world. God had given him a rigidly moral and fluidly amoral Prayer Patriot Proud Boy.

At this moment in which the Acker body remanifested, the glass of Acker had newly melted and reshaped there before Minister Stanley and his son and his friends. Minister Stanley felt hope that Lisbet could be brought back to him by God The Master Magician.

Did Mrs. Panther, a spirit of his daughter's same substance, come to his mind then?

We had seen it countless times: God The Asker asking a believer to accept the dawning revelation, daring an unbeliever to sustain doubt. From his first sight of her, Union had assumed Acker was a Presence. He had wondered whether Lincoln knew, whether Woolman knew. Clearly, Woolman did not know, but Union felt Lincoln would have figured out that Lisbet was Mrs. Panther, Mrs. Panther was Lisbet.

Could you shut up for once? Union said to Webb, who was barking nothing about nothing. Union leaned down to show the dog he meant business.

When Lincoln was intimate with Acker, he would have noticed that she was weightless but not in any normal way, that she had the otherworld soap-bubble tensility and leaf-skeleton lightness children once learned to feel through the poems their teachers made them commit to memory in order to cause them to wander Paradise terribly and purely and sweetly afloatalone. Acker was less than the sadness cast by a passing concern. She was a green thought in a green shade.

31.

In their Helltel room Jacob watched Woolman pass his thumb over an area of the keyboard that had no keys. Twice, he tapped there. Somehow the computer screen grew brighter. He made a tiny sweeping movement, which caused half of his mother to appear.

She leaned forward in her chair, silently stared in the direction of Jacob. She lowered her chin, settled her shoulders. Jacob noticed that, despite herself, she looked more kindly upon him.

Woolman abracatapped a third time, producing from the computer a presto phrase of rubbery swallowings. The uncalm face of the little television screen changed expression.

He and Jacob appeared inside the small portal positioned above Marie's head. "You're right there," said Jacob, recollecting that Marie had always dismissed the Ouija-type connections self-evident for any living persons mildly alert to the wayfaring strangers ghosting the same circular paths over time's spirit board.

"I'm here." When she did not receive an immediate response, she said it again, more quietly: "I'm here."

Her face.

How could the currents flowing through this technology slacken the flesh of her temples and mouth and jaw so much? The small bags under her eyes were puffier. The lines at her forehead were scored differently than during the last Skypversation.

And her voice. Wasn't her voice pitched away from her usual threatening tone?

"Got you," said Woolman, fisherman drawing his mother from the depths to this bright pond surface.

Her laughter, which was recognizable as her free and uncontainable laughter in another time, electronically rippled in a kind of gloomy melody. *You got me, after all*: that was what Jacob heard.

Woolman, who must have heard, too, gazed at his father, the who-are-we gaze.

"Jacob," she said.

"Marie," he said, "how are you?" He asked, "Happy? Happy, I hope."

Woolman asked where she was, though he recognized that bench and the shade falling over the iron boots behind Marie's head. She was in Cord. She was at the Lettgood Memorial, a statue of Edith P. Lettgood ringed by benches. At the feet of the model of filiopietism was a bronze plaque.

> "In honor of Edith P. Lettgood
> and the United Daughters of the Confederacy
> heroically preserving respect
> for the Anglo-Saxon civilization of the South:
> this memorial erected June 3, 1918."

"Where am I? I'm nowhere, I guess."

Woolman said, "Mom. What the fuck? You think I'm stupid? You're right here in town. We could walk four blocks and sit next to you—and Edith."

"Watch your mouth," Marie said.

"Why?" asked Jacob. "Why avoid us?"

Edith lifted one of her iron boots, lifted the other, set them back down: the overresponding eye of the computer caused Edith to move, Jacob thought, or a branch swiping at the sun, or his brain, a head full of marbles and moths, tricking him.

"You're not being fair," Woolman said.

By accident, Marie now tilted her laptop in such a way that they were talking to a different side of her head and to Edith Lettgood's newly polished and handsomely proportioned leg. In preparation for the memorial's inevitable media moment, some festival volunteers had shined the whole sculpture, which increased Woolman's agitation.

"For Jesus' sake," Jacob said, "listen, you two—we've got us all here and that's what matters."

"Leave Jesus out of it, Jacob."

"All right. You're right. Leave him." Jacob didn't say that he was pretty sure leaving Jesus out of it was a good policy anyway for the three of them.

"What is going on, Mom?" asked Woolman, thinking, What're you going to say that you don't want to say to our faces?

"I miss you," she said. "Not you, Jacob. Don't miss you—"

"—much—" Jacob said.

"Not *much*."

Woolman and Jacob could see the bandages on her wrists as she reached toward the screen to pull it into a better position.

"I miss you. Can't stand you. Isn't that crazy?"

"See, Jacob?" Woolman was asking him to see that the atomized materials of their exploded family still hovered above the bombsite. "'You got to move'—that's what Lincoln and I used to sing, Mom. You remember us singing—right? 'You got to move.'"

When Jacob and Marie were younger they had both liked the Stones' version of the old African-American spiritual. When was that? Jacob wondered. Why was that?

The screen flinched. Jacob noticed that Woolman's fingerprints covered the glass, and that made him curious whether he was also seeing Marie's fingerprints.

"You got to move," sang Jacob, and Marie sang the repeated line with him, "You gahh-ahht to move."

You can't let lost treasures hold onto you like they can keep you there—they can't, thought Jacob. They can't. You take them with you. They take you with them.

Her face. Her staring, confronting face. Jacob did not feel as self-conscious as he might have in another circumstance. During the ceremony Skype created, he could fix his attention on her face, and she would hardly notice.

She had noticed though.

He had passed the Oujia-eye of his heart over her, and had summoned from her something she now said, despite wishing to withhold her every word: "I'm supposed to do something I can't do."

Woolman, who thought he had learned the song from Lincoln and Acker, realized he had the faint pilot light of it always burning in him. He sang, "You gahh-ahht to move, chi-i-i-i-ild, you got to move."

"What is that?" asked Jacob. "What are they making you do, Marie?"

Woolman felt irrationally sure now that the three of them could sit together at Lettgood Park. For at least a few minutes they could roost there. He asked, "Do your wrists hurt?"

"Carpal tunnel," she said, turning her arms like a glove model. Jacob, joining in her amusement at the term, could recollect the lightness they had known in loving. Carpal Tunnel. She would be thinking, *Dark in this tunnel!* or *Let's take another route, Jacob.* Or she would move her lips to his silly thought before he would uncrate it in self-delight: *Can you dig it?*

She did not then say what Jacob expected, nor Woolman. Affectless, she said, "Most of me has turned to stone." Her elbows out, hands in stolid fists, it seemed she might hurt her own immobile face, and both men felt she was asking herself to stop her processes of hardening. She was not asking them.

"When will you get the bandages off?" asked Woolman.

The Skypeverse pulsed, swallowed the futureless light it had emitted.

"You're in therapy?" asked Jacob with a fulsome smile that was a risk.

"I should be," she said. "You should be." She did not say, We could be. "Don't you think your dad needs a head-doctor, Son?"

Would that help? thought Woolman before he actually said it, "Would that help?" which caused them laughter more thawing than any he had heard since he was a small child.

Into the holiness of their cheery truce, Marie said, "I hear the bitch killed herself at the festival yesterday."

32.

Woolman asked Jacob, "Are we going to try to explain to her?"

Marie told them she already knew about Acker offing herself and, only a few hours later, onning herself. "Word I got was that she staged the whole thing—a little performance artist show for Cord—and for Woolman here."

"You can't—"

"You shouldn't talk to him like that," Jacob said. "He's hurting and you can see it. Or. What? Something's wrong with you. You're not you."

"Thought she'd get herself some attention," said Marie. "Pretend to bring some attention to Cord—make folks call to mind Lincoln's death, act like she gave a damn about that boy. And she got nothing, am I right? Not what she was after, anyway. The attention. The shock or pity—or applause."

"You got no idea. And you're a fuckin coward talking shit to me but not to my face," said Woolman.

"What *was* Acker after? Aren't there things a decent person never does?"

"You'd know, huh?"

"All right now. Enough." The role of family peacemaker didn't suit Jacob: he could perceive that the role made him ludicrous to them.

Something like heat lightning pulsed on the screen and in the faces there. Light flickers to life or dies within us but in looking upon each other's artificial faces we hardly notice, we notice less and less. We forget how to surveil as we come under surveillance by repeatedly checkmarking, "I Agree" at the bottom of the User Agreement.

"Okay, all right." She bowed her head, brought her hands to her eyes in order to wipe tears away. "I need to know something from you, both of you."

Jacob heard her saying to herself, *Don't. Don't.* He wasn't imagining, he was remembering. Even when he first met her, she habitually mumbled on a falling inflection or muttered on a rising inflection the one-word firm self-instruction, that pitiless self-warning, *Don't.* Early in their marriage when she became more conscious of her habit, she thought she restrained her obsessive repeating of the self-cutting word. Her effort was so ineffective that he could hear her donting in her most inaudible outpushes of air.

"I—we—want to see you. We can talk about what you need," Jacob said. "But why like this?"

"You two. You've found something, I can tell," she said.

"He's different now," said Woolman. "However he was, he—you can see—he's changed."

"You don't see too good," she said, but she looked at the diminutive Jacob on her computer screen where his image seemed to have peeled off yet remained coherent. She thought, He *has* changed. Absolutely, he has changed.

Jacob and Woolman's heads moved close. In a version of a comedy team face-off, they grimly looked at each other. Their grins broke into smiles, which charmed the irreal Skype-space they shared with Marie.

"I need to know—"

Jacob said, "We can come to you."

Woolman said, "We can. Can we? Can we?"

Her hand thrust forward, blotting her face out. She loudly breathed through her nose, she sniffed back tears she would not allow to flow from her eyes. Woolman and Jacob could hear her sobbing, her failed efforts to breathe, her huffings and gruntings as she threw punches with their names.

33.

In the early evening Acker visited the Helltel. She could almost perfectly hear the last-day festivities culminating. The fiddle and singing competitions reeled and ripped and caused her to move her body and to lightly seep where her own bullets had tapped her for flowing blood.

> Now, first I thought a snake had got me—
> it happened dreadful quick—
> 'twas a bullet bit my leg,
> and right off I got sick.
>
> Came to any wagon load
> of ten more wounded men,
> five was dead by the time
> they reached that bloody tent.

As she knocked on the door of Room 209, she thought, Alice—what a long sleep you've had.

The Mister Rounceval and Bunny were Alice's attentive caretakers. They had checked her into the room where at dinnertime the buoyant stew of their dead parents still floated into and out of sight like the collapsing white face-flesh of fish surfacing in a pot at full boil. The Mister and Bunny had explained to Alice that in every season the first hours of darkness made their deceased parents hungry, and in the season's full moon, voracious.

Greetings all around. A holiday tin of homemade fungusy cookies was opened with difficulty. The Reagan-era air escaping from the tin gasped, Heh? and Bunny said, "We'll need tea if we want to get these old snickerdandies down."

When the whistling kettle quieted, empty teacups chattered on plates as if a nervous, seated jury tuning up. Self-whispering came from the doorframe and the window frame—the wordsounds *iti iti*—unrecognizable to Alice, but not to Acker and Bunny and The Mister Rounceval.

The old building settled more ruinously into its out-of-plumb substructures, the resonant crawl spaces and clotted pipes murmuring their own soundages, *neti neti*. Union liked untranslatable object murmurations, reminders that the darkest and brightest universes were merely flying decks of cards, the edges slicing the air into utterances.

The boiled-white eyes and the gasping mouths of the Rouncevals and Duviviers, the parents of The Mister and Bunny, created a fog-retreating atmosphere in the room. Alive in the afterlife, they liked partying with other alives and, when they must, with the after-death dead. *Ititi* they said hungrily to one another, and often, quite urgently if barely audibly, *Neti neti neti!*

Bunny offered a report about Alice's "style of healing." She said, "Alice here holds together. But, you see, the poor dear starts to feel that won't last. And so—it doesn't last. She has panic attacks. She can't breathe."

"Constipation occurs," said The Mister.

"Painful evacuation, to be exact," said Bunny.

"Poor dear Alice, we are talking about her—you—in front of you—her."

"Alice," said Acker, "alicealicealicebloatedalice, may we discuss you? Of course we may."

"We tell her, 'You are or were young. Are. Were. Listen to the festival,' we tell her, 'everyone out there is was is happy and you can feel—'"

"—all the urges of people who want to execute a gliding run and turnaround, to commit the perfect music-crime, make murder pure," said Acker.

The Mister asked, "You have that outside in, don't you?"

"Give a freshly filleted person a fucking break, would you?" Acker said with a haddock-eye glance that was neither unkind nor kind.

"We open the windows wide," said Bunny. "We sit with her friendly. We talk with her kindly. She's a sweet person probably—potato eye—sweet pea. She could be. Was."

"Who knows?"

"Who knows?"

"She could have been."

"Who knows—but there's no urge there sometimes."

"At other times, Alice has urges upon urges, the poor dear."

Bunny said, "Heard you suicided, Ms. Acker."

"Yeah."

Itiitinetitinetineti, said the house in sadvoidness.

"Looks like it didn't take," said The Mister.

"Didn't *what?* The whole operation went fine. Killed me one hundred percent."

"Lord-life-is-a-mystery," said Bunny, who learned the long word from her mother Cleantha Duvivier who needed reading glasses and hearing aids and orthotics but went without all her life and afterlife.

"Like having a cesarean section done," Acker said. "With bullets."

The confused despair on Alice's face obliged Acker to say more: "I'm offed—and over it. You listen to the fiddle music, Alice, the singing? Some of the singing's so amazing, you take in some so deep you gotta off yourself to get over the goodness."

> *Give me some of that soldier's joy—*
> *you know what I mean—*
> *I don't want to hurt no more,*
> *my leg is turning green.*
>
> *Give me some of that soldier's joy—*
> *ain't you got no more?*
> *Hand me down my walking cane.*
> *I ain't cut out for war.*

"She closes the window every time we open it," said The Mister.

Acker abruptly pulled the pillow out from behind Alice's back. "Alicealicealice, little hostage, you like this rat trap more every day, don't you? And me, your bestest jailer, you love me more when I'm cruelest." She fluffed the pillow, calmly said, "I'll fuckin kill you if you close that window again—ever." She positioned the pillow exactly where the good softness would offer Alice the most solace. "There, that's more comfortable than a crushed windpipe, now, isn't it? Isn't it?"

"I won't. Close. The. Window."

"Pay attention, lover. Get your rest. Eat your food. Wipe your mouth, your nose, your pisshole, your asspit, keep your feet on the bath mat. Walk around the room. Sit on the toilet longer. Shower. Change your clothes. You've given her consignment clothes, I see. You like my muumuu, Alice? Get her a couple muumuus. There's one with a radio-tower pattern. Want some fuck-loverly flammable apparel, Alicelove? I'll bring it. Brush your hair more at the nixmirror, brush the old brush with the new one, brush the mirror with the face in the mirror. Pay attention—that's all I'm sayin'. So many risen from the dead—there's always new white robes on the clotheslines and hoods on the heads. There's beasts newborn in the church crèches, new snarling dens of Fox-moloch Dee-dubya Griffins. Pay attention.

Keep your windows open. Windows *open*. There's people hanging from swing sets out there, Agent Alicealicealicealiceaagentalice. You heard them creakingswaying? Can that be right—hmm? Hmm? You know how this goes—don't hang a young man where the children can't find him. Make your purpose plain. Hoist him up, set him swinging."

"I won't close the."

"You're fuckin right you won't. I want you to hear the world you can't have, and see the swing sets."

At the window, Acker asked something of the empty sky that it couldn't answer.

"Alicealicealicealice, say 'I won't close the window'—say, 'ever.'"

"I won't close the window," Alice said. "Ever."

"Whuuuut-ever. My bad. I meant, say 'ever' and don't say all the rest."

"Ever."

Young termites groaned in every boardfoot of the Helltel, and the poached Duviviers and Rouncevals plished through the rusting pipes. *Netineti-itineti,* said the room, and, crisply, *Neti.*

"Miss Acker," said Bunny. "It's my belief that you should make some kind of announcement, because there's folks here who'll want to know what to do about your death or what to say about your—your—"

"My time in the afterdeath. I hear you, Bunny. Some people here want you to stay dead and the ones who want you to be alive—but living in a more definite way—get freaked if you don't make up some kind of explanation."

"Townsfolks here care."

"You're right. They do," said Acker. "This town is a live sex show in the Sean Hannity Pizza Parlor, and the extra-pepperoni customers care about seeing you banging away at the why of it."

Bunny answered, "Our folks don't want the truth—I'm not saying that. They want what they want."

"She's right, don't you think, Alice?"

Union could answer Acker now for Bunny and for Alice and for all. He knew that if she would listen hard he could be heard. He remembered how our people in Cord had been genuinely good people who liked to hear our hearts beating beneath our hands for the prayer, the vow, the birth, the baptism, for the grade school pledge, the saying of grace, the high kicks of the cheerleading team, for the matriculation, the bootcamp, the parade, the teardown, the storage bin, for the obituary description, the artificial grass rolled onto the gravesite berm, for the shovel toss and "Taps," for the anthem.

> *Well, the red blood run right through my veins—*
> *it run all over the floor, dripping down his apron strings*
> *like a river and out the door.*

> *He handed me a bottle, said, "Son, drink deep as you can."*
> *He turned away and then he turned right back*
> *with his hacksaw in his hand.*

"Where is Agent Dookian?" Alice asked.

"He's out there," said The Mister.

Post 9-11, when we were killed by our own collapsing twin Babels, we wanted to seem to be alive, to seem to be renewed and seem to act righteously. That lasted six weeks. In the six years after that time, we got used to making worse everything we might've done wrong to ourselves and to everyone we liked and loved and almost-loved. After the Bush years, after those years wandering the desert like a plague of scorpions pouring out over the world, we wanted most of all to openly despoil ourselves and everyone who loved us and whom we might have loved.

"Is Agent Dookian going to be all right?"

"Oh, dear," said The Mister.

"No?"

"Agent Dookian?" asked Bunny, "You want to know about your boycicle—but you haven't eaten your snickerdandies."

"Good as pureed chickenskin," said The Mister.

Post all-systems collapse in 2008, we wanted to seem to be alive, and we elected a president who could feel his heart beneath his hand. A flawed man, too Black for some of us and not Black enough for some others, but one who meant the allegiances he pledged. We felt hope—most of us here in Cord felt real hope.

Hope with an expiration date of about six months.

By June 2009 we hated Obama, who was beyond us in his patient and decent and compassionate nature; his resistance to corruption was beyond our tolerance; his resilience was beyond our comprehension: a seeming-tame, sleeves-rolled-up street organizer but a not-your-negro-pushover. We hated his darkasdarkestAfrica wife for her stare-right-through-you eyes and her muscled arms and her fierce, authentic love for her husband; we hated their undimmed, bright children, unmistakenly happier than our white-bright but dimming children. Disliking them was not enough for us in our self-despoiled Foxdens. We hated their intelligence and those perfect-teeth smiles and crisp, ironed clothes, even their frisky dogs, friendly, unhungry and happy and exuberant in the official White House photo ops. We thought of reasons to hate the new government health plan Obama proposed, and reasons to not read about or understand it, and we could have called it Republicare because all of us over forty had seen Republicans repeatedly propose programs like it, but we named it Obamacare, because naming matters to us more than reasoning or reading or understanding. We thought of reasons to hate Biden, Obama's bromantic vice-president, the president's biggest fan, servant to the Black-on-blackface overlord. Joe Biden had never tried hard enough, we felt, though we saw how he tried to be better than he was and than he had been, and we hated the grail-chasing goof for trying too hard.

By November 2016 we hated Obama for insisting we wait eight years before we completely put aside all our own actual decency and our own soul-deep compassion and hard-earned patience and unfaked tolerance. We hated Hillary, who had threatened to make us wait another eight.

Acker handed Alice a tissue for her running nose.

"Alicealicealicesloppyalice."

The idea of a Black man as president was so impossible for us to sustain for his entire first year, we wanted to see him killed; if that was not possible, we wanted to be killed—but killed better than on September 11, 2001, and better than on September 25, 2008, the crash date for the economic collapse. We wanted the happy poison-meals the gilded people live on, the supersize emoluments that go down good in your executive tower suite or on your personal country-club golf cart or protected by a fake injury from the Arlington rain in your golden four-poster bed at TV time or with your stormy pornstar companion after taking a knee at a Florida resort Cracker Graham church service you left early for a bonesaw lesson with a Saudi prince.

"Are you listening to everything out there?" Acker asked. "Some of that singing and fiddle and banjo playing is pure-D-purity coming out of the almost-human-Cordite-Christian Psalm Book. So purty you can feel the music cleaning the air everyone breathes." When she looked more closely at Alice who moved her limbs now as if she were enclosed in an enhanced interrogation coffin-box, Acker thought, America, look at you now: the larger you make your prisons, the smaller your prison.

Alice heard the festival through the open window: the holy human barking and howling that blended noise with sound.

> *Give me some of that soldier's joy—*
> *you know what I like—*
> *bear down on that fiddle, boys,*
> *just like Saturday night.*

Give me some of that soldier's joy—
you know what I crave—
I'll be hittin' that soldier's joy
'til I'm in my grave.

"Say I'm right. Alice. You love me. We're wedded wholly, aren't we? You are innocent. You are pure. You are promising. You are loved and loving and alive and lively. Alice-caged-up-alice-fucked-over-alice-stockholmed-slow-smoked-alice. An hour ago I was dead as a dickwad and what traveled out from me hasn't entirely traveled back—I'm on a mudsled is what I mean."

"You're—"

"I'm right. Say it, Alice."

"You're—"

"You were. You were as light-voiced and light-boned and light-borne as him, as made for flight as my Lincoln who was *supernal*—and you wouldn't have the first idea what that word means though you know the feeling—to be with someone who has come somehow to you from as nearfair and farweird away as the crests of crater rims on Mars."

And Acker told her what it was like, what it was like to die and return. Acker explained to her that there's a question about whether you do return.

"You don't return if you don't become dead. You have to know the dead feeling." She said, "But you already do know, Alice. You came here, saw that Lincoln had been murdered, helped cover it up—with Dookian's help and with so many other people's help. You must have gone home after the cover-up—where is home for you, Alice? You grew up in Trump country, right? The Virginia Fall Zone of

172

the Coastal Plain, no, the Tennessee Cumberland Tableland, no, the westward Highlands. No?"

Acker fluffed the pillow. She calmatively held it over Alice's head in order to show her that all the fluffing was for her, Agent Alice Bracco.

"And," she said, "you must have felt you killed yourself right here in Cord, you became dead because of what you did, and you went home where everyone could see that and not say it, but where everyone that you knew—the birthers, the white supremacists and misogynists, the hoaxers and false-flaggers, the Foxfuckers and the Mercerators, the Kochsuckers, the Popists and Bannonpealers, the Putin accomplices, the religious extremists-terrorists—your father, mother, brother, sister, uncle, aunt, cousin, papaw, mamaw, grand, great-grand—all of them would feel good about being soul-dead if a person as intelligent and kind and alive as you could come to Cord and do what you did."

Acker placed the pillow behind Alice's trembling head. She kissed her on the lips. Slipped in a little tongue. And on the tongue some blood, her own.

34.

The Soldier's Joy Festival closed up at 5 p.m. The musicians left after the cash awards were presented. By 9 p.m. the booths, largest and smallest, were taken down and hauled away with the speed people will only bring to bear after a full week of shining up and showing and moving and resupplying the merch day after day.

Woolman told Marie and Jacob that he and Acker had big news to share with them in person. Marie surprised Woolman by saying she, too, had big news she wished to share, and that she hoped they would let her bring wine and cheese and fresh homemade bread to their planned get-together; she said, "Don't act so surprised." Jacob said he had information he would like for them all to have, and he emphasized to them, "Nothing big at all."

The full moon was the fossil-ridged waxing gibbous kind our people have always called a Barnacle Moon, a hitchhiker on the leviathans of darkness. The front door of the consignment-bar opened by itself. Without saying so aloud, Acker and Woolman assumed Union Vedder had decided to attend. He was, after all, the secret-gatherer and secret-releaser in our town, which is no different than any small community of Merikafirst people with the bulging ticks of their secrets swelling on their pates, in their pits and their private places.

When the door closed slowly after them, Jacob asked toward the gleam on the bartop, "Hello? Union?"

"Who else? How black Berlin," said Acker. "How black Berlin" was something she would say instead of saying, "Does the devil sell Bibles?" or "This, too, will pass—not." Her arm closed in para-motherlust around Woolman's waist as she said to Marie, "Shall we say it's good to see each other?"

"Now why would we do that, Miss Acker?"

"I suppose we might wish to make everyone else less frightened," she said, taking the wine bottles from Marie. "Say hello, Woman."

"Hello, Mom. You brought things. You came. In person."

"I did."

Jacob said, "And with bread and cheese."

"I did," she said in self-amazed response to everyone's amazement. "I like that vest on you, Jacob. Is that from the consignment?"

It's true, then, thought every person and presence in the room, that the kind notes in the measure can undo the entire symphony of the unkind, if only momentarily. A slight whooshing sound came from the group's collective relieved exhalation, making Union feel he would give up both living and reliving if he could hear such incalm-outcalm return to the town's breathing.

"I do look handsome, eh?" Jacob unpackaged the cheese and the bread and set them on the bar, the aroma filling the room with sharpness, sweetness. He wiped his pocketknife against the pattern of golden trumpets on his vest, and he carved crude squares and slices, congratulating himself on leaving the bar surface unnicked.

"We have real knives, you know," said Acker.

"Better to leave them be," said Jacob. He uncorked the wine. He hovered over the offerings.

From behind the bar, Acker brought out wineglasses, showing everyone an old blind-pour trick in which she closed her eyes, held the bottle high over her head, a glass behind her back; glass by glass, she poured the long red stream behind her back without spilling a drop; and, in the same instant, she bellied up to the bar and flipped the bottle and the last empty glass over her head so that they landed one beside the other for a final pour.

"I call this Wicca chapter to order," she said. She opened her eyes.

"Ha-ha," said Marie.

"Ah! Ah!" said Acker. "First order of business is the new visitor we've captured, killed, and now must bury in our pages."

Acker opened the cash register in order to withdraw the little wax envelope containing the butterfly brought in weeks ago by the presences Razan and Yusor Abu-Salha, young women in stylish headscarves who had come for the Soldier's Joy Festival, for the music of the young and the very old and the haint-ancients, and for the fried food and the uncased guns, the booths of the bark-bone-wood-coal-root-hide-clay-cob-twine-pinecone craftsmen, and, everywhere, The Beast paraphernalia, including hijab and niqab in appealing digicam arid-environment camopatterns. Their murderer, a self-identified white nationalist evangelitrumper, had explained to investigators that the headscarves had triggered his uncontrolled rage, that he was a stable genius who had been maliciously provoked. What moves through Merikristians now are the human-hating ghosts of humans; "they asked for it" and "she asked for it" and "I alone know" are considered sound Jesus-approved justifications for deadly cycles of violence.

Woolman and Jacob and Marie lifted the bricks from atop *The Silence That Is Within Us*. Together, they made a little Jenga tower that could not easily be knocked over. They rebalanced. With a light touch, with a little body English, the three of them rebalanced. As if a breeze refreshing the room, Union opened the book to the appropriate resting place for the butterfly. No one saw him smooth down the pages, no one heard him say, You three—you are more beautiful than we knew—than you knew. No one saw him place his finger on the words "No Encore" and say, And now, a reading from The Book of Betty.

"May I?" asked Marie, who as a child had witnessed the ceremony. She read two lines from the poem, "No Encore" by *Celestrina Neglecta Bettyadcock Lycaenidae*:

> I'm just an assistant with the Vanishing Act.
> My spangled wand points out the disappeared.

Appreciative spitwhats came from Jacob and Marie. The "What? *What!* what …?" caused a chord of laughter in the room so uncannny it might have come from a nest of owlets. Under the influence of the two conjuring lines of poetry, they remembered other tails of dust and gas in human voices propelled beyond them with great force.

A good poem, they all agreed, and Acker said that Brother H, the consignment-bar's deli supplier, had brought another, a *Eurima Nicippe Kathrynstriplingbyer Pieridae*. "Not today, am I right, Siri?" she asked.

Siri said firmly, "Error. Error."

With no assistance, The Book clapped itself closed, and *thfuffl*ed and *ffhitt*ed before quieting under the pressure of the bricks, a truer country to itself than the delivery room or battlefield or hospice.

"I've needed this place," said Marie. "When I was a young woman this place was Minister Stanley's. The consignment items sold so fast you had to practically stalk the racks every week to get what you wanted. The bar was—I don't know exactly. Was it darker?"

"Lots," said Jacob.

177

"And the booth seats were unpadded—and didn't we love to hate Minister Stanley—you couldn't trust him and I'll bet you still can't—"

Woolman said, "He's okay. You don't know him much, Mom."

"Who does? You know Minister, any of you? And did he tell any of us much about himself, and did he ever decide what denomination he was? And wasn't Christ-on-the-cross centered on the bar mirror?"

Jacob said, "A postcard Christ. 3-D."

"Yeah. Our Lord and Christ. He rolled his eyes and grinned and high-kicked if you looked at him just right."

From a certain perspective, Jesus had been a happy crucified man, Jacob recalled. When he and Marie had first been married, they liked to drink beers here where they could have the crazy-high young holyman's refractive company, and listen to townspeople and townpresences who tried on clothing or jewelry or millinery more colorful than they, and posed in the costumes, and spilled and sloshed their questions and arguments, who grunted approval or disapproval but granted each other looking glass nonsense, and gave each other the benefit of the doubt that the stinking fuel of even their most hateful impulses could be burned out at church and school and family table and work station and VFW Post and city hall and the voting booth and Stanley's, too, and not carried onto the rotting, sinking ark of American covenant.

The poet's wand had spangled the room with radiant silence.

"I've fallen in love with Marie," said Jacob to everyone. "And that's not my big secret even, but it's sure not a simple rerun. I've fallen in love totally—again and totally—with my son Woolman. And this town, which I loved plenty and never stopped loving—I'm not at all smitten with this shitpile. But the flies here are family, and

I understand that in my gut." Fairly happy that he had found the almost-right words, he held his arms out to Woolman and Marie, who kindly nodded but did not come to him. "None of that's my secret." Inside him, he said to the disturbance of light in his wine-glass, Union, d'you think anyone'll care about my big secret?

Acker said, "You're about to fuck over the big news Woman and I want to share."

Woolman said, "This is my biggest news ever, Dad. Let us tell ours—and then you can tell yours."

In Marie's eyes, Woolman looked like her and not much like Jacob except in the way he carried his shoulders and back, an invisible burden that had grown heavier with Lincoln's death. Her son's rela-tionship with Acker—well, who the fuck was Acker anyway, and what was she, and how many eons old, and why was it so impossible to name what-who-how she was, and when did naming fall away as a way to get a grip?

Woolman's grin claimed the attention of everyone there. They could see him from a different angle now, and he did not speak yet because he wanted this: to be seen freshly. His posture shifted, his body lifting him out of the room and out of their company, out of Cord, though his folded hands went to his heart in a way that asked for their hearts' closer-than-ever attention. "I'm going to UNCA—in Asheville—it's nothing like here but not far away, you know." When he took up his mother's hand, she did not shirk but held tightly, and when he looked into her eyes he did not see the indifference he had always seen. "I think I'm going to major in Environmental Studies. I didn't get any scholarships but they say I can reapply for some. So. I start in September. The next ten months I can save up some spending money because ..." The sorrow shading Marie's and Jacob's faces stopped him.

Acker said, "He needs spending money, and that's all he needs for the four years. He has a full-ride *Acker Dom-sub Academic Grant*. Right. Right. Definitely right: there is no such thing. There has not been a regular tradition of Dominatrixes funding college for submissives, but there has been a history of BDSM kinkster-aftercare as far back as Betsy Ross and George Spankyouthankyou Washington. Little Mike, add me foursevens. Was that TMI, Siri?"

Siri said, "TTTTMI."

"Anyway," Acker said, "I'm a one-off sadomiracle, not a perpetually flowing holy fount of money."

Marie said, "I wish I could believe you or understand anything about you, Miss Acker. Or that anyone could, but—"

"But I guess you've got to know how this is possible. If I were you—less than clueless—I'd want to somehow know the howsome, the how, or at least the least of the least-how. How is funding for this program made possible, Siri?"

"Collaboration, screenwriting, kill fee. With author—deceased—Angela Carter," said Siri. "*Bluebeard*, full-length feature film. Director, Akira Yoshimura. Release date, January 2020."

"I've received my part of the screenwriting payment, which will cover a full ride (not a euphemism) for Woman. And as soon as I coerce the money from Carter's estate—she was a good friend, and I always fleece my friends, the good ones—I'll cover a bumper fifth year while Woman gets underway with a life beyond all of us nonrenewable and renewable resources."

Woolman said, "I'm going." He didn't want to leave any doubt in his parents' minds or in Acker's. "I'm going. Live in the dorm. Take a full course load." When he said, "I'll wear a different muumuu to class every day," he felt entirely unselfconscious in laughing at his own joke, and he remembered that Lincoln, too, didn't mind putting out the cold butt of a joke in an ashtray of butts.

Acker said, "I didn't mean to say you're more clueless than all the rest of us, Marie. I'm always picking word-loaves and word-fishes out of discourse-dumpsters and trying to fence them, putting them back in, taking them out again, tossing the bones—a hundred years later diving in again for another feast."

Union's boot tip circled in the dust on the floor. Everyone in the room felt in their teeth and gums the effect of the chalkboard-scraping sound.

"This is done, then," said Jacob. "I see you've worked this all out. I see you're good on your bond, Miss Acker. I think I'm—well, I am—I'm—happy."

As Marie followed her doubts where they led, they unexpectedly led away from further doubting.

The center everywhere and the circumference nowhere, a rudimentary dust mandala appeared that resulted in no comment.

Webb leapt out of the mandala, dissolved to motes so fine their coalesced form jumped through hoops of light none of them had noticed in the room until then.

"Whatever your motives, Miss Acker, you're giving him a chance he wants to take." Marie looked at Woolman's hand in hers. "You never once told me you wanted this."

"And that was wrong, Mom. And stupid. Acker said I should tell you. Lincoln said it, too."

Acker said, "'What,' you will ask, 'is the plan for poor, alone Acker after Woman leaves?' Thank you for your kind concern for me, Marie."

As if Acker had not spoken at all, Marie said, "I wish we would let Jacob tell his news. He's dying to tell."

Jacob said, "Nothing big—I already told Marie my news and it'll hold." He said, "I have a question that I have to ask, Miss Acker: You have to tell me. Did you have a college plan for Lincoln, too, did you tell his mother? Did Lincoln and Woolman already know before Lincoln was killed?"

Acker stretched her arms out in the eccentric way that she had once explained as a "yoga-thing," but that all of them understood as the grieving of someone needing to split open her personal envelope of space. She said, "Siri. Answer."

"Yes. No. Yes."

Woolman said, "We loved each other, Lincoln and me."

"And they loved *me* like doors love knockers, like balls love baseball gloves," said Acker who had not asked the two young men to feel her same desire for what she called UBH, Unnecessarily Brutal Horror, but who initiated them into bonding-loving with her while she gave them time to discover their own relenting-loving with each other and releasing-loving with their families and friends in Cord.

"I can't make sense of it," Marie said to Woolman, though of course he had given her a thousand ways to infer that for the sake of love, he had crossed the racial and religious boundaries she helped shore up in her professional career with The People's Dollar and the Americans for Prosperity Foundation.

Acker said, "Our little trio was Black and White and Blood All Over—not hard to know how unsafe that is in Cord."

Only a littlelong time had passed, a lifetime-long half-hour, since the door had swung open.

"My plan—" said Acker, "thank you for asking—is to leave Woman to meet other Womans at school. I want to make sure he graduates in time for his generation to save Earth from environmental apocalypse, global fascism, and the return of Sears, so I will be in contact with Woman while serving as Red Planet Governess for the first Mars settlements; incidentally, Drummer will serve as my Lieutenant Governess."

"Okay."

"Okay."

Marie and Jacob could not think of better responses.

35.

For hour-long minutes everyone stood inside the dust mandala that had expanded in wave-whispers through the four quarters of the room. The hoops of moonlight fell together and apart like a prestidigitator's linking rings. The motedog Webb loped in the air among other enlightened motedogs. The sound of the train and the brief warning whistle reminded Woolman that he and Lincoln could never understand why the engineer accelerated through town instead of slowing down.

Distant from them but still tickering the warped tracks like a bumping phonograph stylus, the train made the *iti-iti-neti-iti-neti* sounds the consignment-bar and the Helltel and the other buildings made: *here-here-not-here-here-not-here*.

Acker said, "Do I hear a motion to adjourn, seconded, thirded, fourthed? We are adjourned without secondthirdetceteraetcetera. Last item: a personal goal before I leave Cord is to have rough sex with Marie and Jacob and Minister and Orelia and Junior and Bunny and The Mister and their dead parents and Arkansas George. Oh, and Brother H. Oh, and Justice Johngee Roberts. Oh, and not Mr. Panther who scares me—and doesn't he scare you? And, if not, why not?"

The doorknob turned.

The door opened wide. Woolman led his father out, and as they stepped into the street, Jacob became a swarm of moths violently flying apart like a pipebomb. The swarm fountained up, rained down, resolved into his father, dissolved into bits of mothfur and mothwing and gutbrittle and the black needles of leg and antennae, resolved into a man something like a mothfather, resolved into an Adamic substance, a temperament, a climate, a misnomer.

"Dad!" said Woolman.

"Well, this was going to be my news. It's nothing big," said Jacob, "and I'm not sure why it matters."

"You're dead."

"I'm—surprises me too, Son."

Woolman noticed, for the first time, that his father's face fit over but did not obscure his faces, and he observed that his father's body swaddled his bodies in a zone of diffusion like the one in which Oppy had lived.

"I'm present, Son, a Presence."

Woolman touched Jacob's shoulder, touched his neck where the weight of his head could be felt. Lightness. With the tight grip of a toddler, he grabbed his father's belt. The belt bound nothing. His father was light as a leaf.

"See that moon? That's the moon that was over me when Lincoln came to see me, after he was killed. I figure it was a few hours after he died." Jacob stared hungrily at the moon, a plate of salt, earth's absolute without qualities.

"Dad, you've been dead that long?"

"Lincoln scared me to death. That's the truth: to death. I went body-down and lights-out, came up as a moth-blanket, beat at myself with my hands for the longest time before I could see they were living. Living hands. Not exactly living, but, well, true-to-life. You know what I mean."

Woolman wiped tears away with his shirtsleeve. He would have wished to see Lincoln when Jacob saw him. He would have wished to see Jacob one last alivetime.

"I don't know why I wanted everybody to know," said Jacob. "I mostly wanted to tell you. Your mother figured it out that day we were caught in the computernet together you and her and me, you know, the Skypenet.

"I didn't want to tell you, but she said I should. She likes the idea that the old Jacob is dead, that the new one might be a better model. She thought you might love me more this way than the old way."

Woolman thought he would not say it; he thought he would; and when he did, he was not sure he had: "I do."

36.

Marie decided to help Acker however she could, to walk her to her apartment in the Helltel, to not let it end here but to give Acker the attention a mother-stranger can give a strange-mother.

"Are you staying to clean up?" Marie asked Acker, who was, after all, responsible for putting the wrong things back in the wrong places in the consignment-bar.

"Yes, Marie. I'm not new yet," said Acker, who had been so many unspeakably beautiful horrors: Blackwinged Vulture, Killer of Light; Rip-off Red, Girl Detective; Sunny California Nymphomaniac; Toulouse-Lautrec; Perpetual Florida; Janey Smith; Erica Jong; Philip Pirrip; Omar Pier Paolo Pasolini; Don Quixote; Thivai, Pirate Captain; Rimbaud; Kathy Ectopic; Berlin, Sailor Insect, Female Voice Telling Story; Pussy King of Pirates; Sister of Abhor; President, National Pain Council.

Marie said, "I'm going to need work now. I've always worked, and I work hard. And—"

"You're hired. Minister and Junior are going to need to replace me."

"That simple?"

Acker looked up at the seven blue hematite marbles on the ceiling. Only seven now. She nodded for Marie to help her call them. The moment they reached toward the ceiling, their hands floated up beyond their control. The marbles landed in their palms. Warm. Marie and Acker put them in a consignment shoulder bag ideal for a young man going off to college.

PART III

37.

Jadia eventually liked the startling ways her host arrived. Sometimes bucked from a mare's-tail cirrus cloud. Sometimes leaking from the deformed knucklebone of a rotting tree. Sometimes the cheery old white woman was a pungent odor pushed near and away by shifting air densities; at other times Jadia's visitor was like a ballooning spider riding her web and flying when the strand broke and then spindrifting upward on warm, rising air strands before exuberantly crash-floating down, encapsulated in her muumuu.

"Splashdown!" said Dot. "I've brought you a BLT and a thermos of black coffee. You hungry? I'm hungry."

Jadia thought, Dot! Is this part of the swamp—all of this—yours?

Dot said, "I've explained everything to you clearly, Jadia. Only this part is my realm. You're in my realm, I always say. I like you here where you're so far inside your selves you look very small from outside your selves." Her voice was childlike, the voice of a bad-seed child imitating an adult. "Look." Dot lifted her muumuu at the waist and let go and the gown sighed.

Jadia was not sure she saw anything—anything at all—under Dot's muumuu. "You taking care of me? Seems like it."

"I am your servant when I must be," said Dot. "I am your master when I may be. Like a bottle of ooze." Sighting Jadia's doubting thought, Dot unscrewed the thermos, misted herself into it in a seething gulp, the lid screwing slowly back on, burping before the last turn. "Genied!" came her swimmy voice from inside.

Jadia could feel that the thermos was lighter with Dot as the key ingredient.

In answer to Jadia's immediate impulse, Dot said, "Don't you dare."

Jadia cradled the container between her hands.

Dot said, "Stop. Please," and when Jadia lightly rubbed the cool outer shell, making a swabbing sound, Dot said, "Please. Do you have any idea how annoying it is to have your bubble or book cover or bottle rubbed when you can't get out? Stop."

And Jadia obeyed. She understood that Dot had made three wishes: that Jadia would obey, that Jadia would obey, would obey.

Stellar wind arabesqued in the vacuum. Jadia stopped rubbing.

From inside, Dot said, "Buzzbuzzbuzz" and "Can't see to see!"

And unscrewed, and poured out in one ungulp, and pooled forth. She splashed the stillness. "Degenied!" she said.

"Good to be free?" asked Jadia.

"Good as a Godburger and cheese fries."

"You're—"

"I agree absolutely. I am richly entertaining."

"Never had me a servant before," said Jadia, though for many decades she had imagined: a man of forty, carved from birdseye maple and, so, dark eyes everywhere on him, on his smoothly sanded fingertips and long fingers, on his palms with deep, long lifelines; on the soles of his wide and strong feet, and on the concavities of his buttocks.

"Where are your feet?" Jadia asked.

Dot lifted her muumuu, amused. "Gone. Time of day, I guess."

"Odd."

"We'll check again later." They both grinned at the easiness with which feet stay or go.

Jadia's Pinocchial man had a bare head and open face of weathered wood. Ears lathed so finely they seemed translucent. Close-grained and willing mouth and lips. If you could name a whispered prayer a man, this is the man you would pray to whisper-name.

Her finely articulated servant Marion.

Marion would do anything she asked.

Lithe as child playmates, Dot and Jadia jumped to the ground and said, "Pussy!" with no other thought than that they had landed perfectly catlike. In only ninety-nine days in Ephesus Swamp, Dot had taught her many magic words. If they wished to have the wind undress them, they sang that sudden-stripping sound, "*Soooothoo!*" And to be redressed but more breezily and slowly, "*Dthoodthoodth.*" Dot reminded Jadia that The Book in Stanley's-consignment-bar had always quietly sung when opened and closed, that it could be willed to sing and that it sometimes sang of its own will.

Dot said, "I have a sister in The Book, in the early pages. Someday someone will open pages twenty and twenty-one, and she'll come alive like euthanized sisters should. I'm not sad about her at all anymore, about snuffing her. Some oneday she'll fly off and out, out and out and out beyond all nets."

In the air above them, their clothes followed. Jadia whispered "tiddidy" to make her shoes dance on the floating cloth, and, since there was fairydawnlight, shadow footprints walked where the two women walked.

"Bee-EL-teecof-fffee!" said Dot to bring the sandwich and thermos to them. Not quite within reach, the items needed to be more kindly asked, which made Jadia and Dot giggle hungrily, thirstily.

They would not talk about Lincoln, though he was the charged electrical differential between them, the imminent sheet of flame.

Dot said, "Tell me about Marion," because, of course, she could penetrate.

Oh. Marion. Oh, my Marion, Jadia thought. Am I going to share you, my pretend friend?

Dot said, "I had one—a summonman, I mean—and what is the harm in that?—he wasn't good wood like yours. Oh. Ha! Ohhhh, ha!"

"He made you laugh?"

"No, I'm laughing because of his material." Dot giggled to herself, which aroused the air of her entire realm. "The Count was made from ruined cotton socks and leather gloves, and tightly stuffed with BBs."

"I've seen that before! Like a Labboarddoll."

"Like that," said Dot, his double-knit nickname, Count Noaccount, still firmly in her mind after years of holding him near and casting him aside and letting him collect her in his tippling, magnetic arms and legs.

"Mine is—" Jadia was struck by how innocently and readily she talked to Dot and, in fact, to herself during her months in this realm, this new home. "Mine has eyes everywhere on him. And wide open and the grain of them surprisal." Is that a word? she wondered.

"Is that a word?" asked Dot, and from somewhere in the woods an honest surplice crane rather formally answered, "Noun."

"Mine is Marion. Came without a last name."

"Sold jug-cider and firewood every fall? Hand-hewn pinestand along 211 where it hits 701? No sign? No price tag on the cords or gallons or quarts?"

"That's him." How could Dot read Jadia's fantasy memories like that?

"I call mine The Count. Hefty. Pliable. Comes when I call him. Only visits as long as he wants."

"My Marion does like that!"

"Tick tock!" said Dot.

"Tick tock!" said Jadia.

They leaped up onto the tree branch that was Jadia's bed and bench. They stretched their girlgull necks and meowed and mewed hungrily.

They passed the coffee and the sandwich back and forth, slurped as sloppily as they pleased.

Out of the world's hurrying stream, they took their time in settling in, in sharing the mysteries of Marion and The Count.

The Pinocchial man's fingers had clicked on the handlebars of her bike as if male clave and striker clave in rumba rhythm. Neither his clever mouth nor lewdlovely, kind eyes ever closed.

The Count, exactly the right large-doll size, had slight give to him. A touch, a brief embrace, a thrust, a night with his cheek against Dot's chest left appealing, unsettling depressions in his materials.

They brought their dolls out to play. In this realm of The Passages, they could play for as long as they wished.

38.

We knew Mr. Panther and Mrs. Panther walked into the same area of Ephesus Swamp every evening in April, as they had been doing for the past five months. They entered the slash pine collar around the swamp. His headlamp was the light of a solitary firefly in vacant darkvastness. His stride was not long; the conversation between him and his flying companion was animated: before they walked more deeply in, we could see and hear them.

Folks would report that they saw other lights and afterstreaks of light glide, twinkle, promenade, disappear inside the swamp's dark stains of ash, black gum, and oak; they heard wordseeds and wordshells unshucked, crushed, disgorged by other hard-tongued creatures of air.

A few times, Union and Webb followed Mr. Panther and Mrs. Panther. Union swore Webb to secrecy about what they observed: that Mr. Panther had a mission in the swamp. Webb, for the price of red meat or strong black tobacco chew in his bowl, would instantly break his promise and would offer something like, If you saw the goddamned shitshow I think I might've smelled-saw-tasted—hope to jeeee-EEzus didn't but couldmight've, couldn't've, might've, might'not've—you'd understand why human fetuses gnaw their own furry tails off before they're ever born.

Not long after they first became aware of him, Acker and Woolman had discovered that if you gave Webb a discarded vapetube—they called them Juulbones—he would morph into a doggolem of non-stop self-talk about how human skin continuously dessicates and sheds a pervasively airborne human pollen; and how feet on the ground cast no shadows though they concede endless information about the walker's journeys; how the human scent of sleepdribble, hair, and snot and car seat smegma and tears and unwashed fingers more or less explain the human trace. When he was hyperhopped up, Webb would recite all of Waltdog's *Leaves of Ass*. (If you guessed there was no such masterpiece, you sorely misguessed, wanderforsaker.) A glint of green under his eyelids, he would taste every precious, precious ring of sound in the yawping poem that he would recite only for his own enthrallment.

During most of the Soldier's Joy Festival Mr. Panther had more or less disappeared into the dimness of his bar booth where he kept company with Mrs. Panther from midmorning to midafternoon.

She would fly into the consignment room and bring him a bauble, something of conversational value.

She placed on the booth table one of Dot's consignment corsets the size of a light aircraft fuselage, unfastening it with her skilled bill, climbing into and through the cloth and bone before taking the whole thing away in effortful flight.

She bowed her head to clink a wedding ring muzzle off of her, and she read the inscription inside to him: "*Bring me.*"

"Bring me!"' Mr. Panther said, and answered, "Amen."

Mrs. Panther sang, "I thee wed."

She flew forth to the bins, flew back, asking if he would like a rubber cigar, but brought him a real one, an Oevsky Especial over sixty years old and still in its fancy black wrapping.

"May I?" she sang, tearing away the wrapper, nuzzling the stale robusto, snipping off and consuming the cigar cap.

He asked, "Match?"

She took into her bill the wooden match he offered, and she struck it against the rough table surface. She held the ash-stick, rotated her head in the crook of smoke so he could take in her lustrous face, her lambent eyes. In the bar mirror Christ shook out his bloody hair and winked approvingly.

They had fallen and flown in love. They had courted each other in the old ways of mud and pond courting, that is, in the happy exchange of parasites and gut flora and mood disorder and foodmania, in all of the delirious trusting transcommunions. They happily, imprecisely altered each other's course through the woods, and cast before them the knocknicking slatesounds of dice striking baize.

He took her on drives in his Volkswagen bug to the nearby farming communities of Ammons and Hedgecoke and Little Bogle and Fazenda. She flew into people's homes and brought him their unopened personal mail, their printed church programs, their child drawings and reminder lists under magnets on their fridges; she read all the faces on the faces of the fridges. She brought him the magnets with the best inspirational advice: Guns, don't shoot children, Ask my mother-in-law, Death does not taste like chicken.

If one asked, investigator to investigator, "No one home?", "No one home," said the other, "ever."

If one asked "So?", "So?" asked the other, with no need of answer.

The tale of Mr. Panther and Mrs. Panther was appealing to Union as a storyteller who made distinctions between depiction and description. He favored a dead-end story like the story of Minister Stanley and Lisbet and Orelia, of Minister Stanley and Orelia, of Junior Stanley and Minister Stanley, of Jacob and Marie, Alice and Mr. Dookian, Eddie and Eedie, Jadia and Lincoln, Lincoln and Woolman, Lincoln and Acker, Lincoln and Oppy and Woolman and Acker, Oppy and Earth, Alice and Acker, Dot and Cord, Lincoln and Cord, Acker and Cord, Union and Cord, Once-Cord and Now-Cord. Though a storyteller's head full of dead ends did not add up to the depiction that people recognized as the memorable realities of a story, Union believed it did add up to the description that people could always recall as the elusive dream of a story.

39.

The Soldier's Joy Festival Board met at the consignment-bar for the Profits, Problems, Planning after-report. Junior noted the record ticket sales profits and the Samaritan sponsorship percentages; with the Roberts Rules of Order permission of Pamela Hayes, he asked to speak about Problems and Planning as one item.

"All in favor," Pamela said, and said (and wrote) "approved" before receiving unanimous assent.

Junior said, "Two islams came. Walked away with bags of camo."

Pamela asked, "You're aware they're not called islams? Did they pay for their items?"

"Oh. They paid."

"Noted."

"There was the suicide incident," he said.

"We cannot have a repeat of that travesty," said Pamela, writing her own words into the Board minutes.

"What happened happened." Minister could not exactly say that he was sure the suicide had traumatized the festivalgoers. Hadn't they thought it was a performance? No, they definitely had not. Some probably had.

"Do we have a clear record of suicide complaints from festivalgoers?" asked Junior. He waited for Minister or another board member to answer.

Pamela Hayes asked, "Am I supposed to have the answer to that?" She wrote, *Following an ignorant comment and an ignorant question from Junior about the Problems agenda item, discussion proceeded to Planning for 2018.*

What had happened?

The small town roared up from the gasoline thrown onto it by Acker's bloody self-sacrifice performance in a town square as square and fair as any ever portrayed in a tale of fear and horror in a sleepy southern Piedmont hollow.

Roar! said the small town. *Roar!* said the small-town crowd. *Roar!* was the sound, the snarling sound of the small-town crowd in the small town where bedsheet brownshirts felt sorely put down like they felt in all their small crybaby towns all around here. *Roar! Roar!* said the white-hot hate states and the hot-white neighbor states raging and roaring and rallying around a squeaking, slime-ringed, squirmy orange bath toy that the bawling, wailing crowd took for a gringrinchy savior. And, after all the barking and teeth-baring and slobber-splashing, there was the roaring, the roaring, the deafening roaring, and the crowd of look-alike incelligans whimpered in weltering rage that Merika no longer let it roar.

People in town talked about the shooting as something that could have been worse if bullets had strayed. Accidental and fratricidal and domestic-incident and suicidal deaths by gunfire were so commonplace in armed-to-the-teeth towns like Cord that it had become acceptable to have more gun-home deaths and, naturally, more mass school-mall-church-town-square-deaths occur not too long after the shooter was identified as a quiet-keeps-to-himself outsider, after the blood of the lamb or the wool of the wolf-in-lambswool was washed away, and after the cleanup of the site-of-the-killing memorial flowerpile and the usual pile-up of emotionally indifferent Twittermuttered thoughts and prayers.

The techno-savvy three young agents needed only a few hours to edit together their i-footage of the Acker incident. They sent the downloadable three-minute final account to what they called SAFE, State Agency Forensic Experts. SAFE would share the information with ICE, the Homeland Gestapo that liked the "flypaper conditions" of free-to-the public annual events in agricultural areas and in evangelical churches. This much was reported in the newspaper, and no one except Acker objected.

Actually, she expressed a strong sense of injury—to the plural of "Expert" appearing in newsprint as "Expert's." She had responded with similar indignation when the newspaper published a photo on the front page with the simple, unelaborated caption, "Local's Opine." The picture showed a spray-painted monkey image of Obama with giant monkey lips sucking his own giant monkey Black dick. Obama's long, coiled monkey tail, really quite beautiful, was a striking snake. On inauguration day of the Trump Reich, this dumpster art had been moved from behind the Perfection Lumber store to a position of honor at the store entrance on the town square so that visitors could appreciate the artwork of our finest young skinhead-Jesusblooded-whitenationalists.

Agents Ward, Shaw, and Melvin had given Bunny and The Mister Rounceval their notice that they would check out of the Helltel in the morning right after the festival ended. The Mister asked if they would like to visit Agent Alice Bracco, but they could not think why, though they were staying on the same floor and three doors down.

"She's sitting up now but she's weak, vulnerable," said Bunny. "She's alone, not feeling all there. A visit from friends might lift her spirits."

"Constipated," said The Mister, regretting that the word did not communicate his compassion for Alice's condition. He asked, "You young men have something better to do?"

As the three took the stairs to their room, Bunny reproved The Mister, "Leave them be." She took the corners of his shirt collar into her fists, let go, and gave him the check-hook-punch that always put his upper body where she wanted it when she needed him off of her after sex. She said, "They won't last."

A sucker for poeticoital allusion, The Mister had always liked when Bunny offered him the sweet, cold plums of William Carlos Williams' poems. He said, "But they're so beautiful where they are."

"Agh, we were all beautiful once," said Bunny.

40.

The three did not check out the next morning. Apparently they left in a hurry during the night, taking only the clothes on their backs and their devices and their rental car and leftover complimentary pillow mints that looked and smelled suspiciously like foil-wrapped mothballs.

There was no evidence in the local or state news that the agents had submitted a report, that an investigation and another report had resulted, that another and another and yet another violent event had occurred in Cord and had led to a dead end that in April would be called a "conclusive report" of no foul play in the matters of Dookian and Alice and Acker.

Bunny threw away the agents' hair products, toothbrushes, clothes, their deodorants and colognes, their microwave pizza leavings and chip bags and candy bar wrappings and smashed beer cans.

At Stanley's~~Acker's~~ Stanley's she bartered with Minister for the no-iron shirts and slacks, the luggage pieces, all the items left behind. One of the agents left a watch of some value; one of them left a selfie stick; one, a mega-flashlight named Umwelt AlphaLicht. Minister purchased the selfie stick. He liked the idea of shooting Orelia and him at some future time.

Bunny brought Alice one of the MAGA hats the young agents had left behind. Bunny commented that it was not a hat made in America and not, in fact, a tribute to how greatly things could be manufactured now or ever again, and she said, "If you don't want it say so—Junior Stanley has dibs on it." When she gave Alice the flashlight as an added gift, she explained that she had seen it on TV.

"They use these in the military—the thing can practically light the dark side of the moon."

"Goes on your belt," said The Mister.

"Would you like your belt back, Alice?" Bunny then unanswered her own question: "Not yet?"

And she touched Alice's waist, spreading her fingers there. "Alice? Alice? No belt? Not yet."

Bunny did not say what she was thinking: that a belt or two are handy things if you haven't a gun to do yourself in, and for a murder, a couple belts were the perfect suicide-seeming weapon, and for a wanna-be-slender waist, a belt served as a cinch to meatify yourself, like the butcher-string pulled tightly round a roast.

No longer recognizing her own will apart from the will of her keepers, Alice asked Bunny what day it was, what month, year.

"You always ask that," said Bunny. "Have you met my parents? Have they visited you here? You can ask them anything you want."

Holding the MAGA hat, clearly deciding to keep it, Alice asked Bunny an emotional question that reached far beyond self-concern. Alice was now in the deepest part of the dizzying Stockholm-syndrome labyrinth. "Is Acker—will she—will she be all right?"

"She's Acker, dear child. If she appears in your story, she's there maybecause she just couldn't stay dead, maybecause she was always in your story and couldn't stay hid. You don't know about her."

"I guess."

"Listen, Alice: I meant *you* don't know about her. I know she loves you. She does—love you. And wants to kill you. She hates to love Cord and loves Cord, about the only place to ever give her peace with her asked-for portion of filthing hate. She loves to be hated before she's loved, and after. She's lost Lincoln, and don't say 'I guess,' little vagenius, because you've got no idea how she went into him and Woolman the same way religion creeps into innocent young ones and into the infirm old and loves the lovingkneelers like no one can, both of them, I mean, Woolman and Lincoln, who loved being on their knees for her. Don't say, 'I guess.' Did God love you once, Saint Alice? Then: you know He loved you most when you were one-down, truly loved you as long as you were in that position."

"You sound like—"

"—Acker. I sound like her. I sound like Woolman and Lincoln, who were poems like Acker. I'm pretty sure I sound like every poem I ever knew good. I'm absorptive. The Mister, too, he's absorptive. Say, did he or Mr. Panther give you your bagfellow? No? Not yet?"

Now Bunny rubbed her fingertips over her rheumy two mirrors and gazed through spoked cataracts at Alice. She spoke quietly: "You: now I mean *you:* you'll be absorptive some day. Something'll lift you or lower you with a hard hitch or hit you with enough followthrough to send you beyond you, and when you expect to be extirpated you'll be excerpted extracorporeally. You'll stay and you'll leave like some seed a rukeyser maple sent away, like a you; you."

Bunny looked at her own damp fingertips. Spit. Rubbed her eyes again.

Alice asked, "Did they, the agents that were here in March, did they ask about me?"

41.

The June night breeze lifted Jadia out of herself into faintly pooling and lapping ceiling light trembling out of a wavering source of flame. After a few moments, she was not surprised to hover above that other Jadia on the ground where there was no evidence of the whitewhale Dot or of their pretend friends or of the conversation inside which so many blue- and green-burning words had danced.

The sounds of her son Lincoln radiated through the darkening tree trunks and branches, traveling to her from the nadir-roots: Lincoln talking to the television—"Preach!" he would say exactly like her Grandma Broadfeet; in her family lineage, the word had always expressed everything that needed to be said about untruths from the many so-called truth-keepers.

She heard Lincoln's couch-snoring sounds, the snortings that were so happy-making Jadia had enjoyed sitting near him to hear the laughter released from his air-gulpings.

She found she could more clearly hear the Lincoln sounds if the Jadia on the ground rested her cheek at the intersection of roots while the Jadia in the air touched the tip of her nose to a branch tip. She could hear. She could really hear: Lincoln closing the front door with a boom, apologizing, "Sorrymomsorry"—and how did a young man have that kind of man-strength and how that kind of sincere remorse and how that kind of flawless record of happily booming apart the peace in their small house, which had once been her mother's and father's house? And how did a young man never pick up his feet in his untied fancy sneakers no matter how many times his mother firmly said, "Stop shuffling and you'll head somewhere"?

And stop saying "Sorrymomsorry" if you're not at all sorry. Had she said that, and why, why would she ever take that tone?

Jadia heard Lincoln messing with Mr. Watchim. Lincoln liked to spin the large oval framed photo of Jadia's uncle Judah P. Waltcham. ("Watch him," was the joke, "cause you know he might-could-be watching you.") The hanger mechanism and the weighting of the nameplate (*Corp'l Judah P. Waltcham * Died 1863 * March 15 * Union Victory* Battle of Deep Gulley*) made a full spin possible with a return landing that was only slightly off-kilter. The wall-grinding *curaxy-craxy-craaaxy-craaaaax!* pleased Lincoln from the first time he heard it and each time he dared hurt the wall and dared insult the yoke-eyed, grime-darkened Black man that way for which he had no permission.

Sometimes even before he cranked her prized Mr. Watchim photo, he would sing, "Sorrymomsorry" in his private whisper reminding Jadia of how her son carried her inside him, reminding him of her vigilance, what she called "giving you notice."

His reading sounds came to her now. Jesus Lord, don't bring this on me, she prayed, while in the same moment she prayed to be found by the sounds of his words breaking free from fine and private chambers of hiddenness. She had joked that she never had to ask Lincoln to read out something because he simply could not read unobtrusively inside himself. He would read an email from an Oppyfriend and have to give it out. He would read a place name or a product brand or a proper noun or a funny turn of phrase in a book. He would feel he must sigh it or say it half aloud or scat the groove he felt ran through it as he had done during his Ralph Ellison obsession: "*Whoo LeeWillie, Aldridge, Opelika, Dizzy, Savoy—Shorty—Captain—Dupree—Teddy—Tilter—Terry—Sarah—Dizzy—Whoooo!*"

Lincoln had no real idea of his mother's love for music. At a young age she had started to learn the cornet, but that shining herald of decadence went to her younger brother Aylmer when he hungered for the nakedniceyness of juking valves. "Girl with her mouth embouched always gonna have to blow fires out," her mother said, giving Jadia notice to keep her anger to herself. When Aylmer moved to Medallion, Ohio, for work as a tunnel laborer, the cornet and the Harmon mute were passed down to Lincoln.

All these decades later Jadia had a good ear for the pitches that broke glass in you. Some of life's instruments were like miners' pickaxes—she had read about them described perfectly in Lincoln's favorite book made by Mr. Ellison—aimed at something you couldn't bear the shattering of. When the pick-point lightly hit a private little sealed bottle of bitter memory, it hit with a smothered high note and hit with another and lightly hit harder at the pain.

42.

Mr. Panther and Mrs. Panther left the Ephesus Swamp and walked and flew the road to the Helltel. Jadia, they thought, must have been aware of Mrs. Panther's skilled ventriloquism, though she did not at any point ask that the Lincoln sounds stop or that they continue.

"How?" he asked Mrs. Panther. "How do you know all of Lincoln's sounds?"

She creweled her stark black flying silhouette into the wide beam of his flashlight. She could instantaneously—and concurrently—imitate sounds once she became a Presence in Cord and was no longer the young Lisbet Pluchet. Lisbet had been sensitive to the timbre and riffle and tempo of sound downstream of her own human heartbeat, but she had sung without Mrs. Panther's instinct for the headwater vibrations.

"Husband," Mrs. Panther said, "you have something salty good for us?"

He stopped. He heard the birdsong of *us-some-saw-tee-us*, and understood.

He unpackaged buttery round wafers he called Miltons, holding one in his palm while she perched on his thumb and pecked at the imbedded poppy and sesame and sunflower seeds and salt grains.

43.

The thundering skies of August made the swamp's skin jump. Jadia, sitting on a high limb, called for Dot, who brought her Marion and her own Count.

In their imaginations they flew the Count and the Pinocchial man, who dolphined through the tree limbs, diving and leaping to delight their childmotherwife owners. Noaccount sounded like a chain passing through a ship's hawsehole. Marion's ankles and wrists clatterchattered, his hard wooden tongue chirped.

Dot said, "We can change their clothes later on. We can dust and brush them down. I wouldn't mind one bit if we polished Marion's parts."

Jadia felt the coming storm, the wind lifting her easily, and when she called her shoes from the ground, "shh-shh," they floated up and onto her feet, and fell off at once because her feet and lower legs were nothings. She thought, Am I—or just that part—gone?

Dot said, "We get along so well, don't we?"

Jadia was not sure she felt sadness for the loss of herself. She was not sure she felt aloneness meaner than she had known since Lincoln's death ten months ago. How could there be aloneness anything like that? She felt ridiculous—Lord, she felt crazy—but tender toward her absurdly absent, newly present self, alive and fresh and worthy of—*reverence* was the word that sprang to her mind.

She thought about her son's reverence for the little Mars creature Oppy. How odd and not odd, she had always thought, that Lincoln and Acker and Woolman had this pretend-but-real friend in their adult lives.

Should adults have dolls like Oppy in their lives?

As Oppy explored inches of Martian landscape in weeks, the creepy little rover talked to them (in a teen female's voice—how Siri would have sounded when she was younger). Making discoveries, Oppy shared her otherworld victories with them; during setbacks told them of her worries for her solar panels, for the well-being of her systems.

If Lincoln would have asked Jadia, she would have said, It's all right—isn't all of Cord another world these days?

At times Oppy shared her past about her mother Sojourner and her mother's sisters Opportunity and Spirit, whom she referred to as *collectors* in the amused, somewhat sarcastic tone of a teenage rover; about her younger sister Discovery who had died on the other side of Mars.

Oppy shared her terror during the red planet storms. She shared her excitement about Rosalind Franklin, her 2020 ExoMars sibling developing in the womb of JPL; Roz the nonhuman scientist would identify what the boys called biomarkers and she would navigate Martian wind through new sailing *discomicromovements*. "Joking—not," said Lincoln. Woolman said, "You can be a scientist and still be funny." As far as Jadia could tell, those two young people had never disagreed with each other.

Oppy shared her mission to SADPAR: 1) Sense, 2) Advance, 3) Detect, 4) Probe, 5) Analyze, 6) Report. When Woolman and Lincoln were only six years old, they could recite the whole SADPAR Gospel of Oppy.

Oppy did not have a view of Earth, but she liked the insights of Earthlings, and liked the kind messages that streamed power toward her. She liked the yearly birthday celebrations for her. She had completed her life mission by her third year, and she enjoyed listing her record-breaking interplanetary accomplishments at these celebrations. Jadia was invited to them, and she attended, holding up a candle like the other millions of Oppy's friends the whole earthworld over, singing the Happy Birthday song, blowing out the candle: she and Woolman and Lincoln and Acker standing together in the light and smoke. After the fifth or sixth celebration, she stopped asking why Marie didn't attend. After the seventh or eighth, Woolman told her that he no longer invited his mother.

Jadia wished she had sought out the unapproachable Marie Edwards because she wanted to ask: Should our teenage boys be in this weird obscene triangle with this whatever-woman? Should they be in this childlike, innocent relationship with a six-legged space creature?

Should our sons move so far beyond their mothers?

44.

In Acker's bathtub, standing nakednear, she and Woolman took turns at the Prom, a large dose, and they stoked the volumefire of the Sony CD player, they blew vapor into each other's faces, and they frugged a little bouncing frug to "Falling Down Blues" sung by Furry Lewis, which led to bounding and jumping and landing beautifully and often so poorly the bathroom shook and the beads weighting the curtain-bottom teetled and the plastic curtain rings skittered. Though she was slight as a skein of virus cells, she was muscular. He was as long and heavyset as a full-grown gar, and he was as lithe.

Earlier that morning she had scored his ankles with her teeth and his feet with her nails, and now they bled slightly from the dancing. When Furry, pleased to be on Repeat function, sang the last part, "I'll never see her if I never turn around," and sang all the song again, Woolman and Acker felt inspired to stop, to turn on the shower and sit down in the tub and talk under the warm rain.

Acker adjusted it to cold.

He expected she would do that. Acker's sweet, coercive torturings were prime-number predictable.

Impossibly, she adjusted the tap to extreme cold.

In admiration of her own kinkwork, Acker downsuppled her ass over the tops of his lacerated feet and toes. "Woman, I've hurt you good," she said.

He agreed, "Real good," and wished Lincoln was in this rainstorm with them. He would have sat behind and in support of Acker, his dark arms around her white-frost whiteness. He would have said, "Doggone you, girlie" or "Come to sink and drown" or something else that had gotten stuck in him from a book he read or song he heard.

"Cold."

"Cold," Acker said.

Lincoln would have said, "And clean," because he liked cleanness. He didn't think of the word like others did: he had a notion that cleanness meant the rightness you couldn't find unless it passed through a hard quieting. He loved to use the Harmon mute (Acker called the thing the Hymen mute) with the stem out, though his music teacher had told him he was making a "vulgar amateur's error," that using the mute would affect the mouthpieces he chose and would make his playing sound more like the style of Niles Davis than Miles Davis. He kept his cork-wrapped mute awkwardperfectly sealed inside the bell of his cornet; he would sometimes press his palm subtly onto and off the front of the mute's little mouth, but he would not remove the device. Muted, he could get the unglossy notes and phrases and pale stillnesses he felt the cornet wanted.

Woolman said, "No questions asked?" which was their code for bringing Lincoln to mind, for remembering.

At the end of September 2016, not long after the three had decided to live together in the Helltel, they had placed a one-week free ad in the area newspapers:

WILL REMOVE STOLEN ITEMS FROM YOUR HOME.
NO QUESTIONS ASKED. NO JUDGMENT. NO SPITE.

Without getting approval from Junior Stanley or Minister, they had identified themselves in the ad as The SAS Crew, and gave the consignment-bar phone number. They could not really justify their plan, which Lincoln explained as a civics field trip, and Woolman as community service, and Acker as bandit yoga.

Minister had said, "This could start trouble if you bring things here for sale."

Junior had warned them, "Don't."

On the first days the ad ran, they heard from people in Decker and Fazenda and Ninepin and Ammons and Hedgecoke and Whiteville and other nearby communities. Brother H, who reported his collection of eleven stolen extension ladders, was their first stop, and they asked if they could borrow the long-bed truck that had been so useful to him for over twenty years of thieving. He obliged, helping them load one after another during their first long day of work: Louisville and Werner and DeWalt ladders, twenty-two and twenty-four and twenty-eight feet. He had no desire for stepladders or orchard ladders.

At the end of the day, he admitted that he could not part with his stolen Little Giant, which he proudly showed them: twenty-two-feet A-frame, aircraft-grade aluminum, three scaffolding positions, thirty-three configurations possible. "Look at her safety shoes," he said, and pointed to her big rubber feet. He had stolen her and all her companions from construction sites. (His *Heads-Up* food truck was only a side job that compensated for his poor pay as Cheese Head deli supplier to Mrs. Chambers' Grocery & Deli and to Stanley's ~~Acker's~~Stanley's.)

He understood he should offer an explanation. "Don't tell on me. I stole the DeWalt to try to kill my fear of heights. Put myself on it day and night. And I killed. I really killed. Turns out you got to kill that kind of thing over and over again."

Lincoln asked, "You ever go to high places where you need such a big, honking ladder?" and Brother H said he avoided places like that, always had, and he visibly shivered at the mere thought.

They left him with the Little Giant, picturing him climbing morning and night to the top cap and tapping there, a victory tap; and resting his hands on the cap with a sense of accomplishment; and, eventually, in victory, resting his arms and elbows there for a full minute; and, at last, sitting for a wobblinghighwhile on that 5 x 12-inch apex; and only days later, terrified, needing to start all over.

The dapper deli supplier dressed exactly like Junior Stanley, in old-school Florsheim Imperials and khakis and a tucked-in pastel golf shirt with a neat collar and an appliqué alligator. His spiffy look was not far different than the missionary look he had worn when he had been one of the Security Officers for Franklin Graham, the attentive shepherd eternally concerned for the welfare of his assets.

Before they left him, Brother H brought them two new butterflies for The Book. He said, "Fresh"—he said, "Hard to net"—and they thanked him. They took the eleven ladders to Toxostoma's small fire station shed where the elderly firewoman-emergency-doctor-police-force-magistrate-judge on the premises said she heard about The SAS Crew's recovery program and confessed her own volunteer firewomen would take things from a burning building if you didn't stop them because they planned to deliver them to the survivors. But they grew fond of the portrait-lockets and hand-carved ducks and hardback books and such things, held them too long, way too and worrisome too long. "I never done any a that," she said, with no conviction evident in her seering green eyes. "Never set a fire nor took from one. But Ima tell you, if you find a stolen fire truck, this town here's got dibs, awright?"

The wind chimes—the wind chimes in the hundreds. They were in awe of how many people—good poor-middle-class-poor-poorer-ever-poorer people who had become utterly self-absorbed while holding down three jobs and trying to stay alive on the collapsing bridge between the twentieth and the twenty-first centuries in Merika the Former Democracy—had stolen bamboo and tin and steel and seashell wind chimes from their neighbors because they needed the music or couldn't stand the music, or needed the music they couldn't stand.

Some folks stole back their own wind chimes or what they thought were their own, and they suspended them on their porches and awnings and any other overhang of garage and barn and home, and wired them up in the lowest and highest branches of trees that rang out and bonetalked and sangsawed and crashclicked in even light wind. If they had to face a job freeze or a demotion or loss, if illness came to them or theirs, if the old roofs of their homes or old crumbling water systems in their neighborhoods gave way, in only months these people would be yellowing leaves blown from crossing to crossing.

They never thought to disable their stolen soundmakers. Not one of them thought to do that, and this curious matter Lincoln and Acker and Woolman had discussed many months ago while they crunched together on Acker's sofa and watched the September 26 Clinton/Trump debate, forgettable except for Trump's cokehead sniffing and snorting and grunting while trying and failing to form complete sentences; forgettable except for Trump's relibeling nonapology for libeling Obama with the birther conspiracy; forgettable except for a Never-Trump movement of Merikan evangelicals culminating on that very night, and growing quieter and more quiescent and more appeasing and more complicit and more intermarried with the lewd Trump cult every night thereafter.

"People here like to hear their minds laugh at their hearts," said Acker, and Lincoln asked, "What hearts?" and Woolman added, "What minds?" and they called Woolman's Aunt Cee, a woman with mind and heart to spare, to have a beer and jalapeño nachos with them. At the most crucial moment in his life, Woolman had been a kind of son to Cee. She felt she was not done mothering him. She told them on the phone that she couldn't come, that she liked having beer and inedible food with demons and she liked what she called their demon dope and demon ways, and she said, "I sure could use some time farther from heaven right now," but, she explained, she had a tick on her that wouldn't leave her be.

Acker understood what Lincoln and Woolman and Marie would only learn months later: that Cee was at the end of her life and was going to keep that secret to her last, full breath.

The next day they recovered shovels, picks, and rakes and picnic-table umbrellas in Ninepin; boats, kayaks, canoes, rubber boots, paddles, safety vests at Websterford Pond in Lockbox; and at a decaying three-hole Japanese-garden miniature golf course in Hedgecoke, an extensive weathervane collection that Delfy and Emily Sparks had purloined.

The two women had to be discouraged from proudly naming their robbery victims, the full list of people only slightly more impoverished than they.

"We're taking the vanes away," Lincoln told them. "We're not in the business of putting them back," said Woolman. The two young men instantiated each other so easily because so many things mattered the same to Lincoln and Woolman.

They asked themselves how long the elderly thieves would have waited to do the right thing if not for the ad. They asked themselves if there was more to the story of the stolen goods than met the eye.

Woolman asked the two women if they could take the Sparks' Trump-America campaign signs away and Lincoln asked would they like their lifelike Garden Negroes taken out of storage for yard display.

Delfy glared at Woolman.

Emily said to Lincoln, "Oh, boy, *boy*," yielding to cruel impulses for which the dross and clay of her had longed.

Woolman and Acker and Lincoln affixed the weathervanes atop other well-made weathervanes on house roofs in Hyla Brook and Whiteville and Lolaridge. They talked about Emily and Delfy and, characteristically, they convinced each other that people like the two women were not bad, not actually, not once the coals on their burdened backs could be seen as faint signals traveling fifteen light minutes from Earth.

At a fish camp in Hyla Brook, when they were folding up an inflatable children's swimming pool, a patched and cheaply made thing, Lincoln asked, "Is this really why we're out here?" and Acker said to Siri, "Siri, this is why we're here?" and Siri answered, "Madness?" and Acker said, "Madness," and Siri asked, "Satisfied?" and Acker said, "Yes," and Acker asked Lincoln, "Do you worry about what's coming?" and she meant the oldnew racehatreds, and he said, "Woolman and I talk about it sometimes."

Woolman nodded to acknowledge that the talk never led them anywhere.

Acker asked, "Does Cee ever tell you what she knows?"

"What does she know?"

"Does Jadia—does she ever ask if you're worried?"

"She loves me. Mom understands me—loves me. Really. But. No."

Clotheslines and clothes; storage sheds with cribs and baby carriages and pacifiers and dolls and methdolls inside; yardmarys and yardjosephs and fiberglass deer and reindeer and crèches and crushed inflatable Santas and mules and horses all slightly larger than life-size: they loaded up the stolen goods; at night, they hauled them out to new locations.

In the morning's draperylight, some Piedmont citizens with lively, unlifelike flocks roaming their properties would wonder at their unexpected good fortune, the unmoving herd amazing in size and number.

Before Acker and Lincoln and Woolman returned Brother H's truck, they transported their swimming pool to a place behind the Helltel. They played there for a whole afternoon and evening.

45.

Everyone in Cord and Helmsworth and Whiteville and Cortege was battening down in preparation for Hurricane Florence, which approached only days after the end of the Soldier's Joy Festival. Florence would make landfall on September 14, the television news had claimed.

Watching with her terrible eye closing and dilating, Florence waited, her octopus arms sweeping, her sonic warnings changing over the water. She moved the sky's light and darkness in her changing densities, spilled together the odors and fragrances of the plant and animal life she pummeled, ripped apart, atomized. Her appetite increased as she sucked, sipped, hesitated, sawed.

Acker and Woolman and Jacob and Mr. Panther and Minister Stanley and Stanley Junior and Marie nailed up particle board on the outside of the building after opening the windows to avoid explosions when the strong winds would intensify and the rains would madden the bogs and creeks and streams and rivers. The outermost arms of the hurricane were already tearing at Wilmington, only eighty miles away, and the predictions were unsettling.

They wrote on the biggest board, R HERE & FINE, which was meant to give fair notice to rescuers who had already sent the clear warning that people who stayed were gambling with their own lives and the lives of rescuers. Everyone in Cord, living so far inland, considered the warnings more or less fake news; they did not trust their regular radio and television programming, and they did not like the posts on their media devices preempted by weather reports.

Acker, more superstitious than most Cordites, felt that the Pine family, if they were mounted prominently on the front door, would assuage Florence. She brought the entire Family Pine outside, cradling them in her arms, her fearless-looking, featureless, mythogenic wards. "Oh, Young Pine," she said, worried that in the worst of the storm his head might not hold.

As she and Minister constructed the shelf-frame for the stolid Pine greeters, he asked the logical question, "What the heck?"

She answered, "The Pines've got an Easter Island thing going on, you know. Anything that's just about all head can head off just about all that's anything."

He couldn't respond because, well, he never could know how to respond to Acker. He wished he could. He wished he could ask her things she would know that God tells a select few.

Minister, remembering that Young Pine had been torn from The Family Pine to keep Jadia company, muttered a prayer-wish for Jadia, who would be alone in the storm. Even more worrisome to him was that Dot Doyle, the worst kind of happy shade, might be in Jadia's company.

A group of parishioners from Jadia's church, AME Baptist Twice Born, had searched the expanse of Ephesus Swamp for five months, and, after another five, held a final service for her at the Baptist Pond picnic site, where they placed a hand-carved lazy Susan on one of the picnic tables. The adults felt it reflected Jadia's sense of service. The children liked to spin it in order to watch the circle of small, carved words blur: *Jadia Lennox. Missing. Son, behold thy mother. Mother, behold thy son.*

Minister did not attend the service since he was no longer of any denomination. He rubbed the top of the Pine heads with his hands, another wordless blessing. He smiled, said, "Phantasmic."

Acker pretended she had never used and overused the word. She said, "What God asks ..."

Minister thought of how well he had come to know a great deal of nothing whatsoever about Acker. He asked, "Do I know you?"

In tonally perfect imitation of him, Acker, the magician's priestess-assistant, said, "I am the resurrection and the life."

And this time when he heard the seven-word incantation he knew for certain his eyes had been cleared of the God mote, and that the spirit of his daughter Lisbet had been summoned and was present.

A downdraft of twisting wind made an impeller sound. Gravely as minor gods, the Pine family members bowed.

"Huh?" Minister said to the Pines. O, Christfuck, he said to our Lord whom he trusted none at all. Her singing would be enough. If I could hear Lisbet's singing, thought the man who had so often quoted the Bible instead of querying his own heart, I wouldn't ask to hear more singing ever.

Acker, who had never touched Minister even incidentally, placed her hands, cool and strangely weightless, over his, and when she lifted them off, the memory-impressions of Lisbet that had left him years ago now flowed in the veins on the back side of his hands and in the deep crease-lines of his palms.

Lisbet had landed inside him.

Acker said, "You're right. She's here. In the air. You're here, aren't you, Lisbet?"

In answer to Minister's thought—*How? How?*—Acker said, "My guess is she didn't like the accommodations in The Passages. It appears she hitched a ride with Florence and here she is."

Mrs. Panther offered a wing-sound of greeting though she was not in sight. The wind responded with a gust playful and ominous.

The storm's weird arms churned abyssal wheels of darkness. *This*, thought Minister throwing off the crowns and robes of all the beliefs he had put on, *this I brought on all by myself.*

And Acker addressed the Pines: "Steer us. Steer us through the storm." She was pretty sure she had heard the chorus of Roger McGuinn and Allen Ginsberg and Joan Baez singing those words during stage repairs at a Bob Dylan concert forty years ago when he and they all wore ghostface and sang warbly without windguards on their mics or with any care for forefronting one voice over another.

Minister felt Lisbet leave as light as she had come. She lifted off and hovered beyond his thought, from the nest-lip of his emptiness. In shining insucks and outwhistlings liturgicalming, she sang, "Ho-ol-eee-ho-o-olee-*ho-o-olee!*"

Kind mockingbird. Kind daughter.

46.

Woolman telephoned to ask Marie to be with Jacob and Acker and him for a few hours in Room 202 of the Helltel. Marie did not hesitate to be there, to wait quietly during this moment when NASA was making the last efforts to re-establish contact through the Martian dust storm, a storm oddly in sync with hurricane Florence. From her own perspective, she could perceive the whole melodrama of Oppy's final report ("It's getting dark, my batteries are running low") as silly; from Woolman's and Acker's and Jacob's responses, she could begin to comprehend the losses resonating in this loss. In the short time since Jacob's return, she had crossed impossible distances with her son.

She hovered close behind them at the computer. With no real idea of what she was seeing, she stared at the feed of pulsing, darkening red on the screen. Mesmerized by the stricken faces of her son and Acker, she felt herself travel beyond their place in this small room. Together, they would cross other distances, she knew.

47.

Minister stored his tools.

"Want a brew?" Mr. Panther asked.

Minister asked, "Is there something else I could have?"

"Oh, have a beer," said Junior. "You always say when the devil's at the door, drink a tall one."

"He's never once said anyfuckingthing like that," said Acker.

Junior said, "True."

Minister said, "I'll have a tall one."

Junior brought one to him.

Outside, Mrs. Panther peeked into open seams of window and particle board. Her talons scrawled graffiti over the blank boards. Each time the wind struck, her body huffed like a small bellows made of feathers.

Minister could discern that Lisbet, no longer in him, was specifically keeping an eye on him.

She had left him a second time.

And what about that? he thought. How is a man supposed to know what a mockingbird knows?

And Webb was out there, too, and tracking nothing, since the wind sifted and shook together every possible trace with other traces.

And Jadia, what about her? She was out there with Dot and Eedie and Eddie. Ephesus Swamp had pulled closely around it a rank blanket of churning fog mirroring the imminent hurricane. Minister's and Orelia's daughter Lisbet was fifteen when she had wandered into that swamp at night; when she had not returned the next morning, he had gone after her.

He had meant to call her to him, but from the first step past the Walk sign, he was reminded of mazes, in particular the dense T-forms of stylus mazes teachers once gave children as unendurable homework. A pencil with an eraser could serve as the stylus you used to mark and correct and mark your progress, but Minister's instrument at home was a brittle stick of whittled dogwood given him by his grandmother. He was assigned to memorize disturbing stylus poems that were single-sentence instructions making that task and, hereafter, all the tasks of the rememberer more impossible for the rest of his life. His least favorite was, "Your stylus is your style is your style is your style is" and another least favorite was "And and And and And is not a plan, Searcher," and another, "Not three, not two, one true and not several ways through."

What if he couldn't call Lisbet back to him? What if that cruelty was what God planned for him?

Orelia sat quietly in the bar booth that had been designated as Mr. Panther's. Not once had Minister mentioned her, thought of her. From her station in the bar's darkest place, she watched him, listened to him, and thought, *Not once.*

48.

Jacob had said, "I can't stand being in this hotel right now."

Marie said, "We need to be out in the open."

"Where the hurricane can kill us?" said Woolman.

"We need it," said Marie, speaking for herself and Jacob.

Woolman and Marie and Jacob walked from the Helltel to the Lettgood Memorial where they sat on the concrete bench upon which no one in Cord sat, except for Marie who was both a citizen of and a stranger in Cord. At this particular memorial the birds and squirrels never alighted; shadows might slant toward the bench-seat but they would glide past. The memorial was set not quite far enough away from the bloody torchlit past, not comfortably near the tikilit bloody present.

The storm shouted and echoed explosions warning and threatening them.

Marie at last made the announcement she had wished to make days ago. She explained to Woolman and Jacob how she had lost her job all of a sudden.

She had been instructed to identify the illegals at their workplaces in The People's Dollars in her territory. Some had been employed there for more than two decades. She knew them. She knew their families. She had recruited their children into The Seconders.

Many of the illegals attended the Protestant church she attended, only they contributed more than she in money and in sweat equity to keep the church alive. She suspected their political beliefs were left-leaning, more left-leaning now that they knew about the MAGA vigilantes. She had no opportunity to directly observe the political practices of the illegals since they were far too terrified to engage in open political action or speech.

Marie had dutifully compiled the pages and pages of prejudicial material. When she gave the file to her supervisor, she begged him to destroy it or to let her destroy it.

"Everything's better this way," said the supervisor, Thomas Homan.

She asked, "What way are we talking about?"

"Let's say we destroy the files. Huh, what then? You'd be fired. I'd be fired. My wife Ginny, who's worked since '81 for the same bosses at APF, would be fired. Well then? I don't like this shittiness—Ginny likes this, she really does, likes it like hunting bears in their dens—if she got herself fired over this shittiness, the powers that be would go right on—and do you know who she would blame for my life and hers and yours circling the toilet bowl? She'd say the illegals were what done it and would want to know how to hurt them worse even than putting their kids in cages.

"She's my conscience. I gotta conscience works different from los-ers', that's all.

"I'm not saying you're a loser, Marie, but you're sounding like a loser all of a sudden. When we're cleared outta the way, when people like her and me are fired, what then? Well? Well other people'll see this shittiness gets done. And you think those other people'll be only whites? Hell no—it'll be all the colors of people who hurt so much they can't take any more and they want real bad to hurt someone already hurting so much they can't take any more."

She was told that according to the cooperative plan between ICE and the state government, the operation would be efficiently carried out at The People's Dollars, four stores in simultaneous raids. At the busiest time of day, the state police would quickly form a ring around the store lots and the areas immediately surrounding the buildings; the patrol car roof-lights would be on, the canine patrol officers also standing ready. A phalanx of ICE officers, armed with Marie's list of names, would rapidly march inside, other ICE officers would guard the store entrances and all the exits, and the assumed illegal workers and the collateral assumed-to-be illegal customers and store staff would be profiled, confronted inside, silenced with a harsh warning, bound with PlastiCuffs, led to a white transport van. A windowless black van would hold the children.

The entire operation would take forty minutes at a maximum. Media outlets owned by The Pope would be present in order to provide carefully edited footage to other media that wished not to be bothered to cover yet another ICE raid in North Carolina.

She was told that her face and name need not ever be associated with the ICE raid.

She asked if that would be the end of it.

She knew that would not at all be the end of it. During the coming hurricane seasons, Homan explained, ICE arrests in North Carolina would be coordinated with the government and church and charity relief agencies providing emergency care.

She had not been able to imagine that: family members in despair of even having food and water and shelter would be betrayed that way, would be apprehended and would be treated worse than the uniformed crews would treat stray dogs. In the White House Oval Office, ICE officers would receive citations from the Cannibal-in-chief for their courage and would give their best cannibalsmiles for the television cameras, their proud families memorialized in the footage. Marie knew she would be outed and would receive death threats if she did not cooperate. She would have to leave her home and state and never return. When Homan solved her dilemma by firing her, he said, "I don't take responsibility at all."

Jacob asked her if she had a place to stay. She said, "I've saved money."

Woolman asked, "Enough?"

She said, "What—why—is this?"

"A rabbit hole, huh?" said Jacob.

That made her laugh, and made her son laugh in communion.

Jacob said, "We've got to get back to Stanley'sAcker'sStanley's. We're going to be blown off the pavement."

49.

Acker and Woolman reunited at Stanley'sAcker'sStanley's. They borrowed Minister's '87 Buick Regal to get groceries and other supplies. The hurricane winds almost blew the bags from their hands as they brought everything into the consignment-bar.

When Minister asked why they took so long, Acker briefly described the many ways they had fucked in and on the car. "Painful as hell," she said without explaining that during her entire adult life her pelvic inflammation disorder had caused her excruciating pain during intercourse, and, eventually, addictively self-torturing pain in sex that she increasingly needed to be routine.

Lincoln's and Woolman's first experiences of intercourse were with Acker whom they recognized at the outset was the alien-familiar woman in the narcotic porn they and all of their high school peers had consumed. She was of two kinds: the teenrabbit and the milfmouse, downloadable female abstractions, lifelike dolls participating in hyperspeed seductions and consentings-inside-non-consentings, grunting submissions in viscerally explicit viewpoints, hammering assaultive encounters that were less electrically sado-pleasuring for the male viewer if any second of footage failed to intimate the excitements of witnessing all the possible iterations of males engaged in acts of rape.

Acker, who was teenrabbit to Lincoln and milfmouse to Woolman, had seemed fantastically of-the-world and otherworldly to the two young men. The friendship of the two, and the friendship of the three deepened in the worlds and underworlds that they explored.

Acker loved them like they were perfect simulacra of the hundreds of men she had intensely and disastrously loved, usually in threesomes.

She had coerced Lincoln and Woolman into gently desecrating, ungently defiling, controlling, and injuring her.

She loved them.

She loved them for their confused and terrified and willing young hearts. Who, except for Lincoln and Woolman would believe she loved them?

She understood firsthand how the processes of forcing pain and shame on themselves and on her in threesomes and in multiple Peeping-Tom scenarios would move them past self-restriction and revulsion to a pure servitude all theirs because it was impossible to rationalize to others.

We're in love: the three acknowledged how ludicrous it would be to try explaining themselves with the three words: that wordless condition made them feel more deeply in love: at a certain point they stopped saying it to each other because they did not wish to defend themselves to themselves: we're in love: the unspoken but expressed feeling was holy-obscene: we're in love: are you this horrifically much in love?, they wanted to know: *we* are: *we* are.

Woolman, blood in his socks, said to Minister, "Took your car to the Off All Carwash—gassed her up in Whiteville."

Acker, recharging her vape device with Prom, said, "You ever fucked in a drive-through car wash, Minister? Get you a hand polish or a blow dry or free hotwax?"

Woolman stood near enough that he could be enwooled in her vapespirit.

We're in love, he almost said.

Junior said, "Stop. You're going to give my dad a heart attack. Just stop."

The drawer-tongue inside the cash register metallically clucked, clinked, barked.

Union.

Webb.

When Union lifted and dropped the brick atop *The Silence That Is Great Within Us*, paper-winged, blending songs belled. Webb repeatedly jumped up, trying to get some of the poetry to sound inside his nose and mouth where he could read the scent. He liked the flavor of flight through wet grass, of ice-singed fields, of sentry fogbanks. He coughed, which made him laugh at himself, poet-dog not once a man, not once even in eons of remanifestation.

Outside, the members of the Post family knocked heads. Young Pine asked a wooden question of his family. No one answered.

Mrs. Panther stopped huffing and scrawling on the roof and all at once flew in through a crack, flew down, perched on the bill of Mr. Panther's cap, shook herself dry to the tailtip.

The lid of the blackening sky pushed harder against the rattling roofs of Cord. The bar bottles lightly rang each other. The consignment clothes flirted in their racks, the wooden and plastic and metal items in the bins clickrocked backforward.

Shyly, smoke seeped in at the storefront, split into light ragcloaks gliding, slowly crawling around their ankles.

Well, shit, said Union from somewhere half-inside and half-outside their awareness.

This spoory smoke enveloping Acker's debtide was spit-on-chalk slick, Webb felt. Like cold bone embers in a campfire pit. He liked the hissing flutes of what is left. He liked that.

They hammered open a hole in order to look.

Minister and Junior and Marie and Acker and Woolman and Jacob and Mr. Panther and Mrs. Panther took turns glimpsing the burning swingseats and the chains swinging along with the three agents' clothing. Smothering rain came with extinguishing force, as if with intention.

"Union?" asked Jacob, "Is that you?"

You know what that is, Union said, everyone hearing him, no one certain they heard.

The strong winds animated the uniforms Shawardandmelvin had last been seen wearing; their burning leather shoes and leather belts and ties danced wildly in the volatile air.

When the strongest fists of rain punched down, nickering sound came from the fire covering every part of the wooden swing set frame, which must have been painted with some kind of fire-lusting substance because hovering blue light persistently licked at the flame-swirls.

All at once, Mrs. Panther flew out through the hole, and they watched her playfully join the strange puppet show of gamboling fires.

Marie said, "I can't watch anymore."

"Me neither," said Minister.

"And why?" asked Orelia.

"Orelia?" Minister could not find her. He said, "Come out, my love. Please. Come out."

"Fuck my silver nut bowl," said Acker, "Don't change the channel—I could watch this show forever."

50.

After Eedie and Eddie located the decimus bushes under which Mr. Panther's nieces Joan and Karen had been buried, they showed him: the vines climbing the bushes were lynching ropes.

When Eddie tugged the ropes, the two young people's bodies slid out from the shallow graves where they had lain for thirteen months, the knots still tight around their necks.

Eddie said, "It's good you're taking them away from here. They've been restless."

Eedie said, "Yeah. I don't think they were going to stay. But. I'm glad they're leaving with you."

Mr. Panther said, "I warned them. I kept warning them. They're my brother's kids. Whenever he's been put away, they've been mine. I was responsible for them." He explained that there was no mother in the picture, that he was supposed to protect them, and that he was never good at it, not for a single day.

They lived with him, their "Uncle R.P.," in Ferguson, Missouri. They called him R.P. because he was so damned determined they would appreciate reading what he called Real Poetry. In their endless arguments with him that "the shit," that is, the hip-hop and the rap they loved, was poetry, he eagerly listened and enthusiastically judged that only most of their favorite shit was shitty poetry and that most of his favorite shit poetry was shitty, too, but more of his was unshitty than theirs—and how were they going to know without reading his favorites?

He had got them through community college at Applied Technology Services in Sunset Hills, Missouri. He was sure they would launch into careers if the timing could ever be right, and he was happy they moved to Charlottesville, Virginia, where he lived and where he owned a music store, Ace High's Music, a place to work full-time while they decided what came next. Then the nazi-wannabe marchers came there, and Joan and Karen fell in with the countermarchers.

They caught fire. They burned hotter and hotter. Their small subgroup grew from six to seventeen; the group participated in field exercises meant to make them more comfortable with military-grade weapons.

At the time that their little group decided it needed more deadly weaponry, they happened to hear about the no-holds-barred weapon sales at the Soldier's Joy Festival in Cord, North Carolina. Some of them had relatives in Kentucky and Tennessee, and as they took the odd route through both states they found opportunities to camp and even to recruit.

Joan and Karen took on the leadership in the group that wore MAGA hats they overpatched with WRRWUW, the acronym for We R the Race War U Want. At the festival, the group enjoyed full open-carry rights. And they enjoyed the food and disliked the music but not the musicians and not the music-lovers and the food vendors and festivalgoers. They offered every young person there—hundreds of them—free red WRRWUW hats, and they took some pleasure in seeing unaltered MAGA hats lose the numerical competition against their own hats in the crowd. Mr. Panther had learned of their schemes, and in every phone conversation with them he had begged them to not purchase weapons, to not mix with the locals, to keep the damned hats out of sight, to understand, to please understand what he was saying. He only later came to understand that Lincoln Lennox had acquired a WRRWUW hat there. Lincoln felt the hat somehow complemented his new sneakers, and even his mother could not make him take it off.

They purchased the guns for which they had come. Each member of their group bought from a different vendor. Not one vendor refused a sale after the inevitable exchange:

What does that—WRRWUW—stand for?

A joke —a harmless fuckyou—you know: like MAGA.

Oh.

Just some trolling we do.

Oh.

By the time their little group of young adults had left the festival, they were in danger far beyond their awareness.

Eedie and Eddie sent Mr. Panther home with Union and Webb. With absolute clarity, Webb's nosey brain now responded to the scentmap of the whole swamp. At almost every decimus bush, Webb called attention to the rope vining the spikey branches. Within sixty human strides in any direction: more of the horrific fifteen decades of plantings, more of the haunted buried ones never found.

51.

The fire on the swing set in the middle of Sweet Thorn Road had become green fire, which the hurricane wished to taste. During the next hour, everyone stepped away from the view except Mr. Panther and Acker. The swing set, the one on which Lincoln was lynched, had been brought directly from the playground to the town square.

As they stared, the flames refined to an almost transparent blue that threw off tiny cloaks of last color, last heat.

"I wonder where they are," Mr. Panther said. It was understood he meant the agents.

"I swung on those," said Woolman, sitting down between his mother and father.

"Me too," said Junior.

Acker said, "Lincoln, too."

Orelia said, "I swung Junior on them—and Lisbet, too, until she turned five and told me, 'That ain't real flyin'.'"

Marie remembered that in the time before Jacob abandoned them, they would go together as a family to the playground, which they called The Swing Playground because the eight swing sets were, after all, the most of it. She would fling little Woolman out of her arms, and catch him, and fling him again, and say to Jacob, "Your turn." In those days, Jacob took his turn.

She could touch her arm on Woolman's strong back now and find Jacob's arm touching their son there.

Mrs. Panther returned to the roof when smothering sheets of rain came with extinguishing force, as if with intention. The smoke that had come inside the consignment-bar had reclined, dissolved, left behind a sprue stench.

The wind plucked her from the roof and tossed her into the air, and each time she determinedly landed again, she was peeled off and thrown up into new helpless delight. Tumbling almost to the ground, she mocked the sounds of the roof tiles riffling and the town's parked cars whistling through their leaky seals and the *whoa-oh-ooh!* and *upupup!* sounds of children and parents loudly playing on the swing sets long ago.

A blast threw her wings open wide, so wide that they would tear her body apart if she could not be another kind of kitelightness; and in that instant, she thought of how her mother and father flew her on the swings and how her brother would fly her there, too; and, without deliberation of any kind, she became a creature no heavier than one of her pinfeathers.

52.

This was not what Alice expected when Bunny and The Mister Rounceval hugged her, tossed her things into a black plastic garbage bag, and guided her to the elevator at 1:30 a.m. The building shook. "Only a hurricane," said The Mister. They mumbled something she could not quite understand about "special transmutation" waiting for her out front. How kindunkind they had been, the two hardsweet old crusts with whom she had been imprisoned in the Helltel.

Her body and mind atrophied by her extended stay in bed, she felt that something was insufficient about the elevator lighting, that the brass buttons on the operating panel were not sequential and, more importantly, were unresponsive to her touch, that the Emergency indicator on the panel should not be covered with duct tape, but she surmised that her weak condition had made her acutely suggestible. Determined to protect herself in a web of unresponsiveness, she focused totally on the rubber door edges shuddering closed.

She tried to ignore the machine-grease odors secreted through the perforated ceiling tiles, to ignore the ceiling light cooling as it dimmed, the cooling, dimming shadows jittering on the elevator floor. She tried but failed completely to ignore the old-fashioned elevator's rubbery burps of compression. She refused full awareness of the walls covered with dense, satiny black material in flowing curtain folds. Within seconds, the form shadows and the cast shadows of the curtains shifted her posture of indifference. Pairs of bright red lovebirds ornamented the shiny, reflective cloth, climbed ivy on slender twigs so shimmering they might have been vibrating—but this, this time inside dark, verdant ice, was something she must have been assigned to read at a scarifying age.

The elevator did not move. The buttons—2, GL, BL, 1, L, 3, LL—were they all pretend buttons, or did only some of them function? So much of the unrelenting terrible unexpected had happened to Alice, yet this was not what she expected at her time of release: contingency questions that were this unfunny.

Grandly now, the whole chamber rose on a screeching cable braking before seating into a metal collar, and another, and another, and another that was rusty-sounding, and a last that engaged with such finality she felt she must be at the Garden Level. When the light dimmed more, hissgiggling came from inside the curtain-covered walls.

She pressed 1 to no effect, and why not press 1 again, and why the strong superstitious feeling that she should have pressed 1 only once? She had experienced this same feeling when she was assigned the first visit to Cord: that she should not accept; that when she was offered the second visit she should not make that choice, but she and Dookian had hooked up, hungering and lusting, sharing playful episodes of delayed satiation, and so she couldn't help but make the groping choice.

Try. Again.

The voice was not her voice emerging under the pressure of nervousness. She would know her own voice, wouldn't she?

She pressed 1. The lightest things in her lungs were now leaden in her bowels. This is not the Garden Level, she thought. And she felt she must have heard the two words coming from the parentheses of the black curtain folds.

Try.

Again.

The breach in the command placed her inside the kind of night-driving shift occurring when tires reading pavement begin reading gravel.

She pressed 1. She pressed 1, not removing her finger. She pressed her whole body into 1.

The door to the elevator opened.

The man who called himself Mr. Panther stood directly in her path. The palms of his hands rested in a fear-inviting, friendly manner on the handles of his machetes.

She said, "Mr.—"

"Mr. Panther. Remember?" He stepped aside. When she offered a trembling handshake, he turned her palms out, he examined them closely, saying something to her or to another-her-not-there, and smoothly gave them back.

She said, "Bunny—The Mister—they didn't say—"

"Odd old folks, don't you agree?"

"You—"

"You could say I'm your Uberator," said Mr. Panther leading the way to his green VW Bug, a vehicle insubstantial as a soap bubble. She sat in the back, behind the passenger seat.

53.

Mrs. Panther lit at the edge of the hole in the roof of the consignment-bar.

Like fairy tale creatures thrown into a deep well, Minister and Orelia and Junior felt their attention drawn to the blinking eye of stormlight that fluttered as Mrs. Panther trembled there, a good troubled place for being seen a last time.

From all the tales books had ever told them, they could perfectly imagine she would fall in and down and be there with them, transformed, her fiddle and bow in her hands. Lisbet.

When she was a young person and absorbed in music, Lisbet had carried the instrument to The Passage in order to play where Eedie and Eddie had summoned her, made her their friend, held her there for another and another tune.

She left the fiddle, walked home with the bow.

Minister, seeing her panicked expression, had asked, "Lost your boyfriend again?" which was what he always said when she left the instrument somewhere.

And she had returned to The Passage, but had not found her way out.

They were sure they could write this tale—theirs—unfolding now in this way: their Lisbet returning to them as inexplicably as she had gone.

They heard the train passing through town, steel body roaring, pursued by packs of hurricane hellwinds. They heard the pained groaning of the tracks. They heard the crossing alarm.

One hard sweep of broomwind took her. They heard.

They heard the radio tower scream in readiness to come down. Instead of coming down, the tower bowed deeply, and they heard the metal cross-trusses groan.

54.

Mr. Panther put Alice's black garbage bag in the trunk; she was glad to have her clothing returned to her: her uniform blouse and pants and impressive official jacket and favorite business-gray ankle socks.

He lifted before her a blue garbage bag, not quite as full as her own, smaller than her own. He set the little blue bagfellow close to her in the car's backseat.

"Where do you—this is kind of you to—you—you came here about the same time as me, didn't you, Mr. Panther?—we—we—"

She watched as Mr. Panther adjusted the interior mirror to place her in context: her bed-head and bed-face and hooded bed-eyes, and behind her the head and the tail-head of the Obama monkeysnake dumpster graffiti, and a smoldering swing set in the middle of the town square and beyond that the closed arms of the railroad crossing more or less marking the town limits.

Inside Mr. Panther's car the radio's mind-erasing static came on by itself and also the old man's body odor and also the taste of cum or of belly lint or pillow drool or chicken fat sweating out of her own unhealthy gums. On the back of the seat facing her: vomit stain. On the floor mat under her feet: newspaper clippings bulging from manila folders, and knotted battery cables, and opened and unopened Snickers bars, and an overall coating of birdshit.

From bagfellow came a nervous dry fart. Another, noxious and chalky.

"Did they say or—nobody has told me—I don't don't—where—you know—where we're going."

"Depends on where we been," said Mr. Panther, his cleverness triggering self-delighting laughter from him. He was a dark man whom she had thought of as exceptionally dark; that is what she saw in her photos of him, and that was the limit of what she felt toward him.

She wanted to ask about Mrs. Panther, the bird usually accompanying him. And she wanted to know, really wanted to know—The Mister and Bunny had not told her—about agent Dookian—had Dookian recovered from his injuries—did he jump—it seemed he might have jumped from the balcony of Acker's hotel room, but he wouldn't have, that's not how he was—and the swing set—what had the investigations found, had the new investigators found the swing-set arsonist?

She wanted to know—she had certainly never seen them outside their scabbards, and she wanted to know about the machetes—an old man with machetes at his hips, she hadn't seen that ever before. How do you ask about a dark man's machetes—you don't—shouldn't—there must be reasons—you can't—but—

He adjusted his mirror again, apparently wishing for a full view of the bagfellow, which held his nieces' ashes and the fresh clothes he had bought for them in the time when he still held out hope. He said, "The mockingbird—Mrs. Panther—she's a concern of a higher order. What do you say we leave her and take up that lastmost concern you got. My machetes."

"You—your machetes?—you know—you *know* me, Mr. Panther? Like, it can't be—like how? You know everything I'm thinking?"

"Alice, your brain is a large-print edition. A bird could read your brain. A bird *has* read your brain, but you didn't know." He increased the volume of the droning radio, and he made a U-turn before heading them in the direction of the Perfection Lumber store with the Obama dumpster placed in front. He slowed down to look at the smoldering swing set in the square. He passed Mrs. Chambers' Grocery & Deli and the Cord Town Hall and Museum on his way toward the railroad crossing.

The bagfellow sighed out a cheese-rind rank odor. More definitely sinkleaning upon her, the bagfellow's puckered head touched her breast as if to suckle.

Mr. Panther made the *Ding-ding! Ding-ding!* warning sound, and he was pleased to see his silliness set her more at ease.

"You find what you're looking for?" he asked bagfellow.

The little bagfellow made a settling puffsound as Mr. Panther put the car in neutral and somehow also put in neutral the air around and inside Alice.

"You want to know about my machetes? I use these to clear. They're sharper than they look and heavier, and they clear good. If you're looking for a certain thing and certain other things are in your way, you can clear with them. If you pass one blade over another, the sound they make sounds exactly like justice."

As if a cool glass tube melting and noisily turning inside a sleeve of superheated steel, the long train roared before them, the timber-fracturing and track-singeing sounds accelerating through the sluicing radio static.

"You know what they call railroad ties?" he asked.

"No."

"No?"

"No."

The dense tissues of humid air ripped when the train tore them, and the tearing intensified the sense of acceleration. Alice could hear that thunder-within-thunder of the compressed rails and ties, and that, too, heightened the illusion of individual cars flowing into one steel river.

The train moved like speeding film through an overjuiced projector. Between frames, a lovely bird flew into and through a young man sitting very still on a swing set seat, the spars and the beam burning, the child's swing next to him burning, the small basket with smaller versions of the young man flying forward and flinging backward while burning. The fire was directly across from them on the other side of the train. The fire had a sound, *husss hussshhhuss.* The fire had a name, she was certain. The Next Time Fire—she had heard it called that.

What do you call the railroad ties? she wondered. She could feel her skin and flesh lifting in desire toward the hurricane sky, feel her body now so like the train speeding down the tracks, cloth ripping through rings no larger than wedding rings.

"I would like to know," she said, her official agent voice dubbed over her own voice with which she had hoped to speak.

Mr. Panther understood that she would like to know why he had come to Cord; she would like to know in her own heart whether the young Black man she had once seen after he was taken down from the wooden swing set was the matter with this world, with everyone she met here in Cord, with all the Alices and Ackers inside her; what had become of Dookian, would he return, could he ever, should he; were the explicit pictures of her body still on Dookian's iPhone and stored in his Dropbox, and weaponized in the Cloud; what do you call railroad ties?

What was the young victim's name? His mother's name? The name of his town, this town. She could not remember.

The track timbers had another name she was certain she had learned once in a story she and her classmates read in middle school.

She felt her finger hitting an imaginary button, repeatedly hitting it, no response, none. Her movement caused rustling in her companion, her bagfellow date who was nuzzling her breast, her nipple—that couldn't be—What? she thought, but couldn't muster the strength to push the hungering plastic puddle away.

Mr. Panther dingdinged. Watching her finger twitch, he brightly dingdinged, said, "They call the railroad ties sleepers. A ghosty word. Who doesn't love a good ghost story? Makes you wonder how many words in this world are scary beasts no bigger than your fingernail."

The bagfellow seemed to agree. Inside bagfellow's blue skin were the two reasons that Mr. Panther had come to Cord, had unrelentingly searched the Ephesus Swamp. He remembered now that when he took the rotting bodies of his nieces to the Saint Barlaam Funeral and Cremation Center, the Black undertaker, the owner, asked him only one question: "How old?" And forty-eight hours later, he personally brought Mr. Panther the two cardboard containers, no bigger than shoeboxes. He refused the money Mr. Panther offered.

Short of breath and out of balance, Mr. Panther had kneeled on the funeral home's carpeted floor and poured them and his tears into the bagfellow. He cinched everything closed with the golden pullstrings.

He handed back the containers.

He carried the bag to his car where Mrs. Panther waited. She tasted his losses that dusted the skin of his hands and forearms.

"They're still warm," said Mr. Panther.

"You imagine they are, my love. Good to imagine."

Alice began to think that there was no hurricane, that those unnameable forces had moved inside the train, that there were no separate railcars, that no space existed between railcars, that there were several trains speeding after each other or by each other but not on separate tracks, the assaulted sleepers getting not a moment's sleep under the train and the din of the train alarm. The last railcar passed.

"Am I right—about scary words—about how scary the names for things can be?" Mr. Panther asked bagfellow since, after all, a bag-fellow is always open to interpretation. A sagging bagfellow may be awakening happily; a sighing bagfellow, swallowing painfully; an unattentive listing-left bagfellow, listening right.

The dark words emerging from bagfellow followed each other closely over her, scouting, orienting, misaligning, slackening, realigning, clamping, fastening. A lengthening, craving, suturefuse of ants.

He parked the VW upon the sleepers.

The crossing arms closed behind them. The silence of the dark man deepened. The bagfellow eased closer.

A robe of white fire covered them.

The passengers entered the blur.

In order to make a donation in the memory of a victim of racial violence or injustice, contact 334-269-1803, support.eji.org, or mail a check to Equal Justice Initiative, 122 Commerce St., Montgomery, AL 36104.

Acknowledgments

I'm thankful to you for entering the paradoxes with me: Christine Hale, Tony Hoagland, Sebastian Matthews, Rachel Haley Himmelheber, Emilie White, Darlin Neal, Peg Alford Pursell, Cass Pursell, Dale Neal, Kathryn Schwille, Katrina Denza; the Warren Wilson MFA community, especially Ellen Bryant Voigt, Peter Turchi, Reed Turchi, Robert Boswell, Rick Russo, Joan Silber, Karen Brennan, Martha Rhodes, Andrea Barrett, Eleanor Wilner, Heather McHugh, Debra Spark, Sarah Stone, Nina Swamidoss McConigley, Susan Neville, Brooks Haxton, Alan Shapiro, C.J. Hribal, Connie Voisine, Deb Allbery, Tracy Winn, Helen Fremont, Erin Stalcup, Justin Bigos, Rose McClarney, Justin Gardiner, Jeffrey Levine. For the inspiring, generative fierceness in your hearts, I am indebted: Mitzi Rapkin, Elizabeth Holden, Janet Shaw, Chris Burnham, Thomas Burnham, Don Kurtz, Rich Yanez, Todd McKinney, Rus Bradburd, Tina Olsen Hvitfeldt, Bob Hvitfeldt, Kent Jacobs, Sallie Ritter, Rhiannon Giddens ("The Ballad of Lennox Lacy"), the Reverend William J. Barber II, T. Geronimo Johnson, Karen E. Bender, Devi Laskar, Rion Amilcar Scott, Julia Brown, Adrienne Perry, and HR Hegnauer. At crucial reckoning moments, The Weymouth Center for the Arts and Humanities and the Virginia Center for the Creative Arts provided me with space for contemplation and discernment, for which I am deeply grateful.

Permission Acknowledgments

About the Author

Kevin McIlvoy has published five novels, *A Waltz* (Lynx House Press), *The Fifth Station* (Algonquin Books of Chapel Hill; paperback, Collier/Macmillan), *Little Peg* (Atheneum/Macmillan; paperback, Harper Perennial), *Hyssop* (TriQuarterly Books; paperback, Avon), *At the Gate of All Wonder* (Tupelo Press); and a short story collection, *The Complete History of New Mexico* (Graywolf Press). His short fiction has appeared in *Harper's, Southern Review, Ploughshares, Missouri Review*, and other literary magazines. His short-short stories and prose poems have appeared in *The Collagist, Pif, Kenyon Review Online, The Cortland Review, Prime Number, r.k.v.r.y, Waxwing*, and various online literary magazines. A collection of his prose poems and short-short stories, *57 Octaves Below Middle C*, has been published by Four Way Books (October 2017). He has received a National Endowment for the Arts Fellowship in fiction. For twenty-seven years he was fiction editor and editor in chief of the national literary magazine, *Puerto del Sol*. He has taught in the Warren Wilson College MFA Program in Creative Writing since 1989; he taught as a Regents Professor of Creative Writing in the New Mexico State University MFA Program from 1981 to 2008. He has served as a fiction faculty member at national conferences, including the Ropewalk Writing Conference (Indiana), the Rising Stars Writing Conference (Arizona State University), the Writers at Work (Utah) Conference, and the Bread Loaf Writing Conference (Vermont). He has been a manuscript consultant for University of Nevada Press, University of Arizona Press, University of New Mexico Press, Indiana State University Press, University of Missouri Press, and other publishers. Since 2016 he has been a fiction editor for Orison Books. He served on the Board of Directors of the Council of Literary Magazines and Presses and the Association of Writers and Writing Programs. He has lived in Asheville, North Carolina since 2007.